FIRES OF VENGEANCE

When Clem Dawlish and Amos Grant discover a valuable oil field near the town of Carterville, they plan to eliminate the ranchers and homesteaders in order to stake their claim. They create a phantom to head a gang of outlaws and destroy the ranchers. The scheme works and Dawlish becomes a power in Carterville. But another phantom arises: one who would avenge all who had died at Dawlish's orders. Now the law of the gun — and justice — would surely prevail.

JOHN RUSSELL FEARN

FIRES OF VENGEANCE

Complete and Unabridged

LINFORD
Leicester

First published in Great Britain in 2000 by

Originally published in paperback as
The Phantom Avenger by Jed McCloud

First Linford Edition
published 2010

The moral right of the author has been asserted

British Library CIP Data

Fearn, John Russell, *1908 – 1960.*
   Fires of vengeance.- -
   (Linford western library)
   1. Revenge- -Fiction.
   2. Western stories.
   3. Large type books.
   I. Title II. Series
   823.9'12–dc22

   ISBN 978–1–44480–088–3

Published by
F. A. Thorpe (Publishing)
Anstey, Leicestershire

Set by Words & Graphics Ltd.
Anstey, Leicestershire
Printed and bound in Great Britain by
T. J. International Ltd., Padstow, Cornwall

This book is printed on acid-free paper

1

For several minutes the two men in the ramshackle little hut on the edge of the Texas wastelands had not spoken. Both of them were absorbed in the map spread on the table in front of them. Around them, piled into corners and thrust upon shelves, were the instruments which immediately identified them as oil prospectors.

'No doubt of one thing,' the taller one said finally, straightening up, 'this region is crawling with oil for some thirty miles around. Start drilling properly and we'll have more gushers than we can take care of.'

His companion grinned round his cheroot. 'A situation like that just couldn't arise, Clem. We can take care of everythin'.'

Clem Dawlish, big-shouldered and tough, was having considerable difficulty in absorbing the fact that after some ten years of searching he and his partner, Amos Grant, had at last struck a rich oil-bearing region. The time they had spent on the study of geological charts, to say nothing of testing the land itself with second-rate instruments, had at last yielded a result. They had struck oil, yes — but had become practically penniless in the doing. Prospecting for ten years without a yield had battered the Dawlish-Grant Oil Company more than somewhat.

Clem Dawlish, pondering, wandered to the solitary window of the hot little shack — or, more correctly, operational shed — and surveyed the dusty waste spread out before him. It was mainly grass-denuded earth, powdery with the fierce Texas sun. In the distance, at various vantage points, were the ranches of newly-settled homesteaders who, knowing nothing of the value of the ground beneath them, had the fond hope that they might one day turn this sun-soaked wilderness into a cattle region. That depended entirely on the diversion of certain water-courses from up north. Meanwhile the merciless battle against Nature would continue.

'Tens of thousands of dollars' worth of oil out there an' right beneath us,' Dawlish mused. 'An' we're the only ones who know about it.'

'Yeah.' Grant came to his side, drawing contentedly at his cheroot. There was absolute complacency on his round, dogged face. 'I c'n almost see the towers and derricks right now. In a few years we can be the richest men in Texas.'

'Ain't quite as easy as that, Grant. In this region there are a good half-dozen ranches, all fairly well established. We can't start drilling for oil in a big way until we've bought up the land of these homesteaders. And the top and bottom of the matter is — we're broke. We can't afford to buy up anyone.'

Grant frowned. 'Only one way around that — start a company. We've got the proof there's oil here so we ought to find good backers. Only thing we can do. We'll need stacks of dollars to begin the drilling in a big way.'

'Once start a company and we're no longer bosses of the situation, even though we may be the governing directors. I'm no believer in trading a good secret for the sake of money — not whilst there are other ways.'

'What other ways?' Grant demanded irritably. 'You've got to spend money to make it: that's an elementary law.'

'The other way,' Dawlish said, his eyes narrowed as he peered into the distance, 'is to blast these homesteaders out of the way. We can be smart enough not to do it ourselves. Get rid of the homesteaders — raze their spreads to the ground if need be — and then we can take over.'

'And where do we get the money for erecting the derricks and operational base? — to say nothing of the labour we'll need? That kind of stuff don't grow on bushes.'

'As to that . . . ' Dawlish returned slowly to the table and stood pondering for a moment or two, studying the map

4

at the same time. Then he planted a thick index finger on one particular spot in approximately the centre of the potential oil-bearing region.

'There,' he said presently, 'is the heart.'

Grant scratched his ear in puzzlement. The spot Dawlish was indicating was the small town of Carterville, the only generally habitated spot in this entire region. It was indeed the centre of all activity, the town from which all the outlying ranchers drew their supplies.

'Run that,' Dawlish added, 'and we have all the money we want.'

Grant dropped his cheroot to the floor and put his heel on it. The bewilderment had still not left his face.

'Look — what the hell are you talking about?' he demanded bluntly.

'I'm talking about the future. The trouble with you, Grant, is that you're too damned honest. No man can afford to be honest when he has a fortune lying in front of him for the picking up. To keep this oil control to ourselves, run the land that bears it, and find the money to finance everything, we've got to throw all scruples overboard.'

'And mebbe finish up as guests at a necktie party!'

'No reason why we should. I said earlier we'd keep ourselves out of it — and we will. You know as well as I do that in Carterville there are plenty of men who'd willingly shoot down their own families for a few bucks. I reckon we've still enough left in the kitty to be able to use a band of men like that — men who'll carry out our orders and afterwards vanish from the region. We remain in the background and only step in after the clean-up.'

Grant looked dubious. Though by no means an angel he had none of the ruthless notions of his partner. To play safe had always been Amos Grant's endeavour — but here, apparently, there was a field so large that it was impossible to master the situation and remain honest at the same time.

'We'll ride into Carterville tonight

when the boys are around,' Dawlish decided finally. 'Nick Salthouse is our best bet. Quite a number of men follow him around and most of them are pretty good gunhawks — '

'More simply,' Grant interrupted, 'you're planning a reign of terror?'

'That's it — but a well planned one in which we can't be accused of having taken part. Our role is that of benevolence. Feeling very sorry for the terror which has descended we'll step in at the right moment and take over. It won't be difficult anyways: most of the men who run Carterville are born stupid. Whatever the cost and whatever the consequences we've got to establish this region as an oil-bearing centre — There's millions in it, man — millions.'

Grant said nothing. For a moment he toyed with the idea of walking out of the whole set-up, then the thought of the oil yield which was to come overrode his decision. He had to stick beside his dominant partner, no matter what.

★ ★ ★

Nick Salthouse was drinking straight whisky at the barcounter of the Journey's End Saloon when Dawlish and Grant found him that evening. As usual Nick's response to their greeting was surly. He was never quite sure who was addressing him — whether it might not be the moment when some past victim had caught up on him. Nick Salthouse's crimes were legion, though he had always evaded the consequences — and his mode of living was a mystery. He was supposed to be foreman of the Double-Noose Ranch, yet the money he always seemed to possess for drink was far beyond anything most foremen could afford. In every way Salthouse was a law to himself and cared less than nothing for any man or woman living.

'Got time to talk?' Grant asked him, picking up his glass of rye.

''Bout what?' Nick's close-set eyes narrowed suspiciously.

8

'Money — and a job which only you and your boys can do.'

'Okay: what can I lose?'

Salthouse led the way across to a corner table, roughly pulled out a chair and planked himself in it. His half-empty whisky glass at his elbow, he sat waiting.

'There's plenty in this if you an' your boys go about it properly,' Dawlish told him, settling. 'Not just for the moment but for the future.'

'I'm still listenin' even though I don't know you.'

'The name's Clem Dawlish,' Dawlish responded. 'I've been in here many a time along with my partner here — Amos Grant — but mebbe you haven't happened to notice — Anyways, to get back to business, I want a good deal of the land around here for private purposes of my own and the only way I can get it is to be rid of the homesteaders. To buy 'em out would be too costly, so I figgered there's other ways.'

'Such as scarin' 'em to death?' Nick grinned.

'My idea precisely. Have another drink.'

When it had been brought Dawlish continued: 'I'm not layin' down any hard and fast rules on how you should do your job 'cos I think you're smart enough to work out your own plans. Clear out all the homesteaders and make this town unfit for any man or woman to live in safely, and that's the sum total of the job. Naturally you'll need other men to help you. I'm assuming you can get those.'

'Sure I can, but what's the pay-off?'

'A thousand dollars a man until the job's done. When the job is done you'll all have to drop out of sight for awhile until I contact you. Then you can come back into the field and work for me as right-hand men.'

'You aim to run the town, then?'

'That is my intention.'

Nick drank slowly, his none too agile mind trying to sort out the details. Dawlish let him be, cast a significant glance at the morose-looking Grant, and then finished his drink.

'Around here there are some seven or eight spreads,' Nick said at length. 'I guess there wouldn't be much trouble in emptying 'em uv their owners since most of 'em is pretty quiet livers. But what's it for? Why d'you want the land?'

Dawlish shrugged. 'That's my business, Nick. All I want to know is do you agree to my proposition, or not?'

'I'd like t'know more about it. What happens if we get caught? Fust time out we'd succeed by surprise, but afterwards the others might be on their guard.'

'That's a risk you've got to take. You're all of you going to be well paid for what you have to do.'

Nick rubbed a dirty finger along his lower lip, then suddenly an idea seemed to strike him. His close-set eyes brightened.

'Ever hear of the phantom horseman?' he asked abruptly, and the blank stares he got from Dawlish and Grant were sufficient answer.

'The phantom horseman is a sorta

11

legend around these parts,' Nick hurried on. 'Supposed t'be the ghost of an outlaw who wus shot up some twenty years ago and died screamin' that he'd come back. Some of the old 'uns around hereabouts say that there is such a phantom. I wus just thinkin' — mebbe we could make that phantom come true to suit ourselves.'

'Uh-huh,' Dawlish admitted, nodding slowly. 'And make the responsibility attach to the phantom?'

'Yeah. That way we wouldn't get no blame ourselves.'

'I leave it to you,' Dawlish shrugged. 'In any case my partner and I are never to be connected with the business, and if by any chance you let our names slip out you get no pay. Understand?'

'Sure.' Nick was looking pleased with himself. 'Ain't a thing to worry about. I'll work that phantom horse routine to the limit. Before I do anythin' further, though, I wanta be sure of the man I'm dealin' with. Half payment now and half when the job's done. I'll be usin' four other men so that's two thousand five hundred you owe me.'

Dawlish hesitated, but only for a moment. Without satisfying Nick he could not get a thing done so he paid out the money in grim silence.

'Okay,' Nick acknowledged, after counting the notes. 'Where do I contact you when the job's finished with? Can't say how long it'll take, so don't expect miracles.'

'We're staying right here in this town,' Dawlish responded. 'We'll be at the hotel down the street. When you start your reign of terror in this town my partner and I will be the ones to chase you out — at a time and in a way to be arranged later. When you want to contact us tie your horse outside the livery stable opposite the hotel and leave a note under the saddle saying the place and time. We'll be there.'

Nick nodded, said no more, and got to his feet. His first move was towards the bar counter and after a moment or two his various cohorts began to gather around him in response to the brief jerk of his head he gave them.

'Sure you know what you're doing?' Grant asked doubtfully, downing another drink. 'I can't see a gunhawk like that being satisfied without knowing why you want the land.'

'He's got to be,' Dawlish snapped. 'If he tries any funny business he'll find he's got the wrong man to deal with ... Now let's get out of here. Less we're seen around the better.'

They left a few moments later, noting meanwhile that Nick was still in the midst of conversation with his followers. All of them presently drifted to a far corner and there continued their 'conference' in comparative privacy.

'The thing's a natural,' Nick said finally. 'No limits have been laid down, an' I'm not going to tell any of you mugs who the boss is. That way you can't spill anythin'. All we've got to do is clean the homesteaders up, each one of us masked so's we can't be identified, and led by a phantom rider.'

14

'You, I suppose?' one of the men asked sourly.

'Yeah, me — an' if yuh want to make somethin' of it just say so. My job's as hard as yours. I'll start the dirty work off each time — firin' the spread we're attacking. That'll pin the main blame on the phantom rider. You others'll follow on and deal with any of the critters who try to save their ranches. Do what you like with 'em but make sure they can't return to their ranches.'

'Kill 'em?' another of the men asked doubtfully.

'I said there wus no limits, didn't I? We're going to spread the rumour round that the phantom horseman's back and that four honest men have bin caught up in his influence and have turned into killers. These mugs around here ain't very bright anyways an' they'll swallow it. Savvy so far?'

The quartet around Nick nodded promptly.

'Only question now is: when do we start?' one of them said, and Nick scratched his chin.

'Tomorrow night, I reckon — with the Double-Noose as our first target. I'm part-time foreman there and I know the layout. It oughta be easy to knock off. Only old Pedder, his wife, and a middle-aged daughter who never was very bright anyways. Yeah, that's our first one. During tomorrow I'll get a cayuse from some place and secretly fix it up to look like a ghost. I reckon if I wear some old clothes and a hat painted white I'll pass. We meet at Norton's Creek one hour after sundown tomorrow night. Check?'

'Check,' the quartet assented together, and upon that they broke up and went their various ways.

Nick did not follow any one of them. He had suddenly become conscious of his responsibility in this matter, and he was also aware of the disastrous consequences which would ensue if he slipped up anywhere — so he spent the remainder of the evening figuring things out on a sheet of paper, drawing a plan of the position of the ranches, their nearness to the rendezvous of Norton's Creek, and the quickest path to make a getaway. By the time he had finished he was reasonably satisfied that the job could be handled without too much trouble.

The matter of obtaining a horse to become the phantom's 'beast of burden' did not bother him either. When he returned to the Double-Noose that night — where he invariably slept with the other men of the outfit in the bunk-house — he chose a reliable animal from the corral, saddled it without anybody being the wiser, and then rode it back to the day-and-night livery stable in the town until he should call for it. In the unlikely event of an enquiry being made concerning it — unlikely since the horses were mainly his responsibility alone — he could always say it had been taken for reshoeing. Whatever the chances, he risked it — and towards midnight entered the bunkhouse in the usual way . . .

Towards mid-afternoon of the following day, when his part-time foreman duties were over, he made haste into town, carrying with him a considerable amount of folded canvas, a can of white paint, a brush, and spare shirt and pants. Nobody had seen him pack these articles in his saddle-bag, nor did he make any attempt to use them until he had collected the 'phantom' horse from the livery stable, afterwards trailing it behind his own mount until he reached the comparative privacy of Norton's Creek. Here, surrounded by high rockery and not overlooked from any direction he was able to go to work.

It was a longer job than he had anticipated and it took him best part of the afternoon to complete it. By then he had fashioned a complete covering for the horse, somewhat on the lines of the protective suiting used by the mounts of knights in the old days. The finished product was a horse covered from head to flanks in white sheeting, loosely noosed under its body and with adequate eye-slots.

Nick's own outfit was just as simple. Shirt and pants were dipped wholesale in the white paint and then left to dry in the fierce sunlight. The hat was trickier, but by the end of the afternoon it was drying out nicely. Nick surveyed, looked at the two horses hobbled close by, and then he set to work on his long-delayed food and drink . . .

Such was the beginning of the campaign against the homesteaders — and that night after sundown there descended upon the Double-Noose ranch the incredible vision of a white horse and rider, clearly distinguishable in the starlight and brandishing a torch. Henry Pedder, the ranch owner, his wife and daughter, only became aware of the visitation when they heard gunshots. The noise sent each of them to the windows and they were just in time to see a blazing torch hurtling towards their ranch-house with the dim outlines of the phantom horseman beyond.

'What the hell goes on here?' was old Pedder's demand, swinging around; then without waiting for an answer he snatched down his gun-belt and strapped it on. With loaded guns in hand he hurried out to the porchway and then stopped, staring in horror at the rapid hold the blazing torch had gained.

So much he had grasped when his wife and daughter came up behind him. It was at this moment that Nick's four masked henchmen came riding into the scene, guns blazing. Pedder and his two womenfolk did not stand a chance. They were dropped where they stood, old man Pedder rolling down the steps into the yard . . . For a time the air was full of the cries of the furiously shooting gunmen, then, as the entire ranch-house caught aflame and began to consume the three bodies, the destroyers rode off into the darkness and were gone. The first blow in the reign of terror had been launched . . .

The news reached Carterville that same evening, and it was brought deliberately by one of the quartet. He arrived in the Journey's End at the double, perspiring freely and covered in trail dust. The men and women at the tables and around the bar counter looked at him curiously.

'What gives, Harry?' the barkeep asked. 'Somebody gunnin' fur you?'

'Ain't that,' Harry panted, and downed his drink. 'I just seen somethin' plain ghastly. It scared the pants off'n me! The phantom horseman.'

The men and women looked at one another, then one of the cowpokes grinned.

'Better lay off that hooch, Harry. It's makin' yuh see things!'

Harry swung. 'I ain't tellin' just a story! It's true! I wus ridin' inter town, peaceful as yuh like, when I saw the phantom rider. He wus followed by four other riders, but they looked okay save I couldn't see their faces. Last thing I saw was the Double-Noose spread goin' up in smoke!'

'You saw what?' demanded Nick himself, coming forward from a corner table. 'Did you say the Double-Noose?'

'Sure, sure.' Harry downed another drink. 'Go take a look — '

Nick hesitated. So far the plan was perfect. He had arrived ahead of his men, apparently in the normal way, and settled to his evening's drinking. Harry had arrived and said his piece. The other men would come in normally at intervals. Just not a thing to show they were connected with the business —

'I'd better go take a look,' Nick said, his face grim. 'I didn't see any signs of trouble at the Double-Noose when I left it, an' I didn't pass anybody on my way here either.'

'I'll come with you, Nick.' It was burly Sheriff Morton who spoke. 'If Harry's right about this we've got trouble on our hands.'

Nick nodded briefly and led the way to the batwings. In a matter of moments he and the Sheriff were on their way — and inevitably found the smouldering ruins of the ranch.

'Sure done it properly,' the Sheriff commented, dismounting. 'Since I don't believe in ghosts I reckon we can put this down to a bunch of hoodlums. Wonder if Pedder and his wife and daughter got away?'

Nick shrugged, surveying the glowing wind-fanned embers.

'No idea. If they did they'll probably have turned up in Carterville by now — '

'In which case we'd have passed 'em on the way 'cos there ain't any other route to town. I don't like this, Nick,' the Sheriff added. 'Begins to look as though murder has been added to this fire-up. We'd best take a look.'

A long probing search with sticks finally revealed all the evidence which was needed. Three corpses burned beyond recognition were found, with watches and rings for identification. The Sheriff collected what few traces he could find and without saying a word rode back solemnly into town, Nick keeping alongside him.

The atmosphere in the Journey's End was unusually tense when they entered it, far more tense than seemed appropriate for an assembly merely awaiting the report of a search. Then the situation became partly explained as, in moving aside, the men and women revealed a couple of strangers standing beside the bar, their faces grim and their hands partly raised.

Nick frowned to himself and received a puzzled glance from the Sheriff. The two men at the point of a gun had never been seen in this region before, and certainly not in the saloon.

'How's about the Double-Noose, Sheriff?' one of the men asked. 'Was Harry right?'

'Yeah,' the Sheriff retorted. 'The Double-Noose is in ashes, and Pedder and his wife and daughter were caught in the fire. I found their remains. What happened to the bunkhouse boys I don't know: they probably ran for it when they realised they couldn't stop the flames. They'll turn up presently no doubt — '

'I reckon these two guys could do with explainin' themselves,' interrupted the voice of Harry, as he edged forward. 'They came ridin' in not ten minutes ago an' they're mighty cagey on sayin' anythin'.'

The Sheriff moved forward. He motioned briefly to the man covering the two to put his gun away. At that the taller of the two men relaxed a little and gave a hard smile.

'Thanks for that anyways,' he said briefly. 'Mind if I get what I came for? A double whisky?'

'Go ahead,' the Sheriff agreed; then he faced the two men squarely. They appeared to be typical outdoor Westerners, with burned-in brown skin and sun-lined eyes. Their attire did not in the least convey anything — simply riding pants, shirts and black Stetson hats. The one who had done the talking was big-shouldered and well over six feet. His companion, though less in

25

height, could doubtless have given a formidable account of himself in a hand-to-hand struggle.

'Who are you two?' demanded Nick, coming forward, and whilst he waited for the answer he tried to assess the situation. These two represented the unknown quantity in his plans. If it were going to be possible to deflect blame to them he meant to make full use of it.

'My name's Jim Halligan,' the big fellow said, taking his drink. 'This is my partner, Clip Dexter. What I want to know is why the hell we get held up like a couple of outlaws when we step in for a drink. What goes on?'

'Plenty!' the Sheriff snapped. 'Some unknowns burned down a ranch and murdered a man and his wife and daughter tonight. It all ties up with a phantom horseman.'

'A what?' Jim Halligan stared blankly, and the Sheriff gave a gesture of impatience.

'Since you're apparently a stranger around here you wouldn't know about the legend. There's a ghost of an outlaw breaks loose occasionally — bin seen sometimes. On this occasion he seems to have got four men under his sway.'

'Sounds like you're talkin' in riddles,' Halligan commented, continuing with his whisky.

'The thing's true,' Nick put in curtly.

'I ain't sayin' it isn't, but that men like you should believe in ghosts sure is somethin'!'

'We don't,' the Sheriff retorted. 'That's the whole point. My guess is that some critter is pretendin' to be a ghost so's he could settle a score with old Pedder, who owned the Double-Noose. That's where you come in, stranger. Nobody around here had any particular grudge against Pedder. How's about you?'

Halligan shrugged. 'Never heard of the guy.'

'Nor me,' Clip Dexter added. 'We're just passin' through an' it ain't even decent to load all this grief on to us.'

'Can you give a good account of your movements in the last two hours?' Nick demanded, and this seemed to cause both men some thought. Finally Halligan finished his whisky and gave a sigh.

'I reckon not. The both of us rode in from up north and decided to stay here for the night. Take it or leave it: that's the gospel truth.'

'And supposin' we don't believe it?' Nick asked grimly.

'Hold it,' the Sheriff said abruptly, as he saw Halligan's hard face change expression. 'We've nothin' to go on except suspicion and that ain't no use whatever. I can't pin anythin' on you, Halligan, or your partner, but I'm tellin' you to stick around this town until I give you permission to move on.'

'You are, huh?' Halligan's eyes glinted. 'Supposin' we're not in the mood to follow out your blasted orders?'

'You'd better be in the mood, feller. I'm Sheriff around here and I've the right to order anybody to do as I say — specially when murder's bin done. Stay around. If you try and leave town either me or my deputies will bring you back.'

There was a grim silence for a moment. Out of the corner of his eye Nick saw his remaining companions come in through the batwings and drift in various directions; then his attention came back to Halligan as he spoke.

'Since you put it that way, Sheriff, we'll stay put. Guess we're not in a hurry anyways — but if you try and pin murder and fire-raising on either of us there'll be trouble with a capital T. Meantime, where's a rooming-house in this cockeyed dump?'

'Try Ma Kershaw's down the street,' the Sheriff grunted; then he turned to survey the waiting assembly. 'You've had the facts, folks, and we don't know yet who done this job — but we're goin' to find out. It mightn't even be the only attack, so each one of you who has a homestead hereabouts had better keep on the look-out. Like I said, I ain't believin' in any phantom horseman: that's just a gag for five characters who think they can thumb their noses at the law . . . Tomorrow we'll bury what remains of Pedder and his family and then we'll start a thorough search to see if we can find a lead anywhere to the identity of the attackers. I think I've the backing of most of you in that?'

'Yeah, sure.'

'Any time you like, sheriff.'

'Then that's all. I — ' The Sheriff broke off and looked at the batwings as a group of cowpokes came drifting in. They had about them a general air of uncertainty and weariness.

'The boys from the Double-Noose outfit,' Nick remarked, gazing at them. 'Mebbe they can tell us something.'

He remained where he was as the men came up to the bar. They ordered drinks and then turned to look at the assembly.

'Harry told us what happened at the Double-Noose,' Nick commented. 'We've investigated since. Where have you fellows been since the place went up in flames?'

'Walking — and nothin' else but,' one of them growled. 'The bunkhouse caught fire along with the rest of the spread. There weren't nothin' we could do so we just ran for it. Then we decided to double back into town here. All we can do. We've got to settle somewhere until we see what comes next.'

'Not much to tell,' another of the men responded. 'We wus in the bunkhouse but we'd no idea what was goin' on until we heard shootin'. It looked as though the durned place was surrounded. Ranch and barns were blazin' like hell and the bunkhouse had just caught alight. We fired several shots at the attackers, but we couldn't keep up the attack 'cos we tried to stop the fire gettin' a grip on the bunkhouse. When we found we couldn't do it we got out quick — like Jim here just said.'

'You saw nothing of a phantom horseman?' the Sheriff insisted.

'One or two glimpses, but the masked riders with him were sure human enough. Myself, I don't fall for that phantom line. Reckon it was somebody dressed up, and the cayuse as well.'

'Exactly what I think — what all of us think,' the Sheriff conceded. 'Okay, we can't get any further at the moment. We'll begin an investigation tomorrow. Meantime, you fellows had better start lookin' for fresh jobs — and until you find 'em you can help me and my deputies pick up what clues there might be.'

2

But there were no clues. Though every available man helped the Sheriff and his deputies — including Nick and his cohorts — there was nothing that offered them a lead. True, there were hoofmarks in plenty around the ashes of the Double-Noose, but none of them was distinctive enough to make it worthwhile looking for the horse which had made them. The whole search ended in a dead end and Nick inwardly congratulated himself. At the same time he set himself to think how he might be able to finally deflect blame to Halligan and his partner Clip Dexter. Both of them had helped in the search, probably in the hope that there might be something to disprove their own connection with the business.

Altogether, the Sheriff was thoroughly dissatisfied, and said as much after the funeral of the remains of Pedder and his family. Apparently there was nothing could be done until the phantom rider struck again — then it might be possible to move fast enough to nab him and his unknown followers red-handed. So, since Nick and his boys were perfectly aware of this intention, they decided to lie low for the time being.

'Might do worse than have Halligan and Clip Dexter help us,' Nick commented that evening, when he and his cohorts assembled for their usual drinking session in the Journey's End.

'Them two?' One of his followers cast a dubious glance towards the bar where Halligan and his partner were quietly drinking and exchanging desultory conversation. 'Sounds loco to me. This whole racket's sewn up tight between us five: where's the sense of bringing two strangers into it?'

'Because the Sheriff's plumb determined to pin guilt on somebody in the end. We're not nearly finished with our job and the safest thing to do is to get one man, or two, who can get the blame if the worst comes to the worst. I'm thinkin' of the future.'

Nick did not wait to hear any comments. His own mind was made up, and that was sufficient. He waited until he caught the glance of Halligan and Dexter and then jerked his head for them to come over. They did so, glasses in their hands.

'Somethin' to say?' Halligan enquired, in his uncompromising way.

'Yeah . . . Have a seat. The both of you.'

Halligan and Dexter complied and Nick was silent for a moment, weighing them up. He felt he was right in his assumption that their harshly chiselled faces bespoke men who were anything but sentimentalists — men who'd be willing to do things the hard way. In a word, Nick felt reasonably convinced he was dealing with two men whose minds ran on the same ruthless track as his own.

'I'm goin' to take a long chance on you two,' Nick said finally, and at that Halligan gave a grim smile.

'Nice of you. We're not askin' you to take chances. We're just sore at being suspected of doin' somethin' we haven't touched. Be bad enough if we had.'

'Ever been mixed up in trouble before?' Nick asked casually, and at that Halligan's hard smile widened.

'Our trouble's bin to keep out of it,' he said. 'But what's that gotta do with what you were goin' to say?'

'Just this. There's a movement on hand to make a big change in this cockeyed town. Change of control entirely. I'm goin' to let my hair down and tell you that the attack on the Double-Noose Ranch wasn't the work of a phantom, or outlaws, or anythin' else. It was a deliberately planned raid worth a thousand dollars to every man takin' part in it.'

'I like the way you talk,' Halligan said. 'Keep right on.'

'Me an' my boys was responsible for

that clean-up,' Nick explained frankly. 'An' there's plenty more to come. We don't get our money 'til we're through. I'm tellin' you all this 'cos it won't do you any good if you decide to talk. I'll simply deny everythin'. On the other hand, if you feel like stringing along with us there's another thousand dollars each for you when the jobs are finished.'

'How many more jobs are there?'

'Seven more. An' they'll have to follow in quick order so's to keep that old fool of a Sheriff on the hop.'

Dexter asked a question. 'Who's back of this set-up, anyways?'

'A couple of guys who've got plenty of money and won't spill their reasons. They want all the land hereabouts but don't want to pay for it. Only other solution to that is to scare everybody out. If the folks get killed in the doing that's just too bad: they're given time to get away.'

Halligan reflected; then: 'You're suggestin' we come in with you on the later clean-ups?'

'Why not? This phantom horseman routine is a good one an' with careful planning there's no danger. I reckon the pair of you could make use of a thousand greenbacks apiece, couldn't you?'

'Who couldn't?' Halligan asked ambiguously. 'Just the same I'd sooner do my deal with the two men back of the whole set-up. Your say-so on a thousand dollars apiece doesn't convince me. I want it from the man who's going to pay it — then if he doesn't — ' and Halligan tapped his gun-belt significantly.

Nick looked vaguely irritated but he kept his temper — then he suddenly gave a little start. Coming through the batwings with a casual air of prosperity were the very two men who had been under discussion — Dawlish and Grant. Both were attired in black suits and smoking cheroots, apparently at peace with the world in spite of the fact that by now they must have known of the turmoil their scheme of elimination had created.

'Them's the two you want,' Nick

said, nodding towards them. 'The bigger one's the boss.'

'Yeah?' Halligan studied them as they moved to a distant table in a corner. 'What's their names?'

'Big one's called Dawlish; the other one Grant. I wouldn't know what they're doin' around this region but that don't matter as long as they pay up. Since they've tipped up half I reckon they'll be good for the remainder. Mebbe I'd better go over first and break the ground for you.'

'Mebbe you had,' Halligan agreed, with his taut, unfriendly smile.

By no means certain whether he had taken the right gamble or not Nick got to his feet and wandered over to the bar counter. Dawlish and Grant both saw him coming but deliberately avoided looking at him. He ordered a drink and then edged sideways, finally speaking out front in low tones, near enough for Dawlish to hear him.

'I've had to sign up a couple more

men, boss. This business is bigger than I thought.'

Dawlish knocked the ash off his cheroot and appeared to be talking to Grant.

'Did you have to knock 'em all off wholesale at the Double-Noose as you did? You've sure started a pack of trouble in the town.'

'If Pedder and his wife and daughter got in the way of our bullets that wus their fault,' Nick growled. 'Fact remains I've got two new men who'll be useful — Halligan and Dexter by name. I'll send 'em over.'

Nick went on his way, nobody any the wiser that he had been holding a conversation with Dawlish — and, getting the signal, Halligan and Dexter rose together and ambled across. Since there was nothing against them speaking to the two crooked oil men they made no effort at secrecy, beyond keeping their voices down.

'Nick's been givin' us the set-up,' Halligan said. 'You've started somethin' that's pretty big, Mister, and the more men there are workin' on it the better. Y'can count me and my partner in. Nick tells me the figger's a thousand apiece.'

'There are enough men on the job as it is,' Dawlish said curtly, turning. 'Don't need any more.'

Hard blue eyes studied him. 'Up to you — but remember my partner here and me could make things almighty difficult for you if you sidetrack us out of the little job.'

'Meaning that I either take you both on at a thousand each or you'll talk?'

'Right!' Halligan ordered a rye and waited. Dexter, for his part, was already drinking languidly, and missing nothing.

'Better do it,' Grant murmured, as he saw Dawlish was undecided. 'I don't know who this stranger is but he can gum the whole thing up if you don't talk nicely to him. I could have warned you long ago that this would happen. Once you start trouble it has a habit of growing.'

'Oh shut up,' Dawlish spat under his breath; then he turned back to where Halligan was standing waiting. 'All right, it's a deal. You'll take your directions from Nick.'

'Uh-huh, I've no objections to that. What I would like to know, though, is what it's all for. What's so important about the land hereabouts that everybody's got to be cleared from it?'

'None of your business,' Dawlish retorted, tugging out his wallet. 'Here — that's half of what you'll get when the job's finished.'

The notes exchanged hands without attracting attention. Halligan counted them surreptitiously, handed half to Dexter, and then looked at Dawlish again.

'There are three possible reasons for your wantin' this land,' he said, musing. 'One could be water and control of a hidden creek somewheres; the second could be gold, though I haven't heard of much yellow dirt in this partic'lar region — and the third could be oil.

Frum what I've heard there's plenty of oil in certain parts of Texas if y'know where t'look for it.'

Dawlish realized he had started slightly at the mention of oil, but he covered himself up quickly.

'I told you it was none of your business, didn't I? You're well paid to do as you're told without asking questions. From here on deal with Nick and never with me. Nick and I have an arrangement for communicating if need be.'

'Okay,' Halligan assented coolly. 'Ain't no need to get excited.'

He jerked his head to Dexter and together they returned to Nick's table. Dawlish stood eyeing them for a moment and then called for another drink.

'Can't say I like the set-up,' Grant commented morosely.

'You don't suppose I'm cheering, do you? Who is this man Halligan, anyways? Where'd he come from?'

'Halligan?' asked the voice of the

Sheriff, and the two oil men started slightly and then gained quick control over themselves. 'You gents enquiring after Halligan?'

'Just wondering about him — and Dexter,' Dawlish said casually. 'I don't seem to have seen them around here before.'

'Not much surprise to that, is there? You're strangers yourselves more or less. Don't come here often, do you?'

'Time to time,' Dawlish shrugged. 'But I was asking about Halligan. Do you know anything concerning him?'

'Not a thing — an' matter of fact I'm more'n a mite suspicious of him, and that partner of his, Clip Dexter. They say they're just passing through, but it seems more than queer to me that they decided to pass through last night when the Double-Noose business happened. However . . . ' The Sheriff shrugged. 'Can't do anything without proof.'

'No, I guess not,' Dawlish said.

'Come to think of it,' the Sheriff continued, 'I didn't see either of you gents around last night. Don't think I'm being inquisitive, but I'm tryin' to account for everybody last night. Can you tell me what you were doin'?'

'Sure,' Grant said calmly. 'We were discussing business in the hotel down the street. You can check up on that any time you wish.'

'Thanks; mebbe I will.' The Sheriff grinned a little. 'I'm sure going to be one unpopular feller around here before I'm finished, but I've got my duty to do. Be seein' you around.'

He nodded and went on his way. Dawlish looked after him and then his lips tightened.

'Sooner we get some action around here, Grant, the better I'll like it. That sheriff's going to be a damned nuisance before he's finished. When the final clean-up is made of this town he's one who's definitely got to be taken care of. Mebbe I'd better give Nick the tip to hurry things up.'

He ambled casually forward between the tables, followed by Grant. As he passed Nick's table Dawlish murmured a few words. In consequence the gunman presently got up and passed between the batwings to the boardwalk outside. Some little distance away, in the shadows between lamps, Dawlish and Grant were waiting.

'Want me, boss?' Nick enquired, coming up.

'Yes. The way things are going there's more than a chance we might get tangled up before we're finished. From here on you've got to get a move on — clean everything up as fast as possible.'

'Uh-huh. Would it be Halligan and his partner who's worrying you?'

'Partly — but the sheriff is my main concern. He's determined to nail somebody the moment he gets the chance. To make ourselves safe we've got to be rid of him.'

'Simple enough,' Nick responded, 'but the only way we can make a big clean up of everythin' and leave it as you want it — wide open for you to take over — is for me to have enough men to handle it. I'd figgered on dealin' with a couple more spreads tomorrow night — but that'll be the limit with the men I've got. Let me rake in another twenty and the thing's a certainty. Surprise attack will take care of everything.'

'You can have twenty men if you can find them, but I can't pay them a cent until the clean-up's complete. Then, in full control of the whole town, I'll very soon collect what's needed.'

Nick scratched his ear. 'That makes things plumb difficult. The boys won't work for nothin' — an' since they won't you can't get your clean-up.'

'Look,' Dawlish said deliberately, 'this whole thing's a terrific gamble and whether it comes off or not is up to you and the men you get. If it does you'll be amply rewarded, both for present and future. If it fails we'll all be in the soup anyway. It's up to you to get enough men who'll trust you — and me — and make one tremendous clean sweep. The later rewards will make it well worthwhile.'

Nick snapped his fingers. 'Okay, I'll do it somehow, and tomorrow night this town will be in for the hottest visit it ever had. Leave it to me, boss. You'll have to judge your own time to step in and take the reins.'

'Okay,' Dawlish assented, and he smiled complacently to himself as Nick swung away and strode resolutely back along the boardwalk to the batwings . . .

'Think it will come off?' Grant asked uneasily.

'It's got to,' Dawlish told him. 'I keep on telling you, man, that this land's loaded down with oil and wealth. It doesn't matter who gets trampled on just as long as we get our hands on it. Once we're in control we'll do all the talking — and if any blame is needed we'll promptly switch it to these boneheads who are going to shoot up the town for us.'

*   *   *

What plans had been made for the big clean-up, or what men Nick had gathered together, neither Dawlish nor Grant knew. Once they got to their hotel they remained in it, wondering throughout the peace of the next day what was going to happen. Then, towards sundown, they moved into Dawlish's bedroom — which commanded a view of the main street, and waited for something to happen.

It was just after sunset when they did this. Swiftly the night closed down and the kerosene lights came into being. Lights came up in the Journey's End, and here and there the first straggling customers made their appearance. Otherwise all was quiet.

But it was not so quiet in the region of Norton's Creek. All day long men had been arriving at this lonely, little frequented spot, using all manner of detours to reach their destination without attracting attention. Nick's powerful influence in the town, as far as the wrong 'uns were concerned, had been enough to produce some twenty or thirty trigger-happy thugs who firmly believed that this night's clean-up would set them on easy street for the rest of their days. Those who had their doubts were still compelled to do their part. If they did not do so Nick had promised them he'd hunt them up afterwards — and all of them knew what that would mean.

So, with the coming of night, the cavalcade began to get on the move. Every man knew the plan Nick had worked out: each knew which ranch he had to obliterate and which route to take afterwards so as to converge on Carterville for the final onslaught. And at the head of the rapidly moving masked horsemen was Nick himself, complete once again as a 'phantom' with his horse white-garbed from head to flanks.

The inhabitants of the first ranch to be attacked were in the midst of the evening meal when hell descended upon them. At the same moment a second ranch was attacked and in neither case was there a chance at defence. Bullets and blazing torches took care of everything and two enormous fires reared their signals into the night. In some instances the ranch owners and their families managed to escape, but their homes and livelihoods were utterly lost in flames and stampeding cattle.

As Nick had foreseen — with unusual cunning for a man of such low-grade intelligence — the fires were quickly spotted in Carterville and the sheriff wasted no time in hustling up his deputies and as many men as he could find to support him. The odd emptiness of the town — with so many men working for Nick — was something which he noted and could not explain, then he set off towards the area of the distant fires with his followers riding hard behind him.

So the thing developed into a follow-my-leader, even as Nick had anticipated. By the time the sheriff and his men had reached the first fires others had begun some miles away, and so it went on through the evening, until by the time the sweating sheriff had reached the last of the gutted ranches 'phantom' Nick and his men were converging on Carterville.

Here they met with hardly any opposition since the sheriff was absent with most of the available men. There were only the older men and women and children to offer resistance, and against some thirty masked and ruthless men, led by an amazing white horseman on a white horse, they stood no chance.

Dawlish and Grant, from the safety of their room, watched in fascinated silence as part of the town went up in flames, as the windows of the saloon and stores were smashed in, as guns flashed and exploded and men and resolute women too dropped in their tracks. In less than twenty minutes it was all over and the masked invaders rode on their way, still firing savagely at the unwary ones who appeared to challenge them.

But Nick had not finished yet. He and his men doubled back on to the trail which they knew the sheriff and his boys must follow in order to get back into town. Inevitably the two forces met, some two miles out of Carterville, and the noise of gunshots floated back on the still night air to Dawlish and Grant as, with the survivors of the regrouped populace they worked to get the various fires under control by means of endless chains of water buckets.

The effort they had to make was a big one. The sundried timbers of the ignited buildings flared with inferno-like fury — indeed so fiercely it was impossible to save them. All that could be done was saturate the neighbouring buildings and prevent the fire from spreading. In the course of an hour this had been done and there began a general drift of dispirited, bitter men and women into the comparative sanctuary of the Journey's End. Hardly had the assembly sorted itself out somewhat and begun reviving its flagging spirits with drink than Nick and his boys, dishevelled and dusty, began to appear. Needless to say they were without their masks, and Nick without his 'ghost' suit. Curious eyes followed them as they came in.

'Whisky,' Nick told the barkeep, and then cuffed up his hat and looked around him. 'I've sure had a few rough nights in my time but none the equal of this one,' he muttered. 'Looks like the pay-off, folks.'

'Where have you bin, Nick?' one of the women demanded suspiciously. 'Usually you and your stooges are around here most of the evenin', but there weren't no sign of yuh when you was most needed. Or mebbe you don't realize the town's about gone up in smoke?'

''Course I realize it — but neither me nor my boys can be in two places at once, can we?' Nick downed his whisky and ordered a second one. 'We wus tipped off early today that there was to be a big raid tonight, both on the town and the ranches around here. The sheriff gave us our orders and we followed them out. We've bin shootin' it out with the phantom horseman and his followers.'

As Nick well knew the sheriff had been shot dead so there was no possible chance of his story being denied.

'An' how did you make out?' Dawlish asked, coming forward.

'Not so good, I guess.' Nick grimaced. 'Some of our boys wus lost — including the sheriff himself. The phantom rider got away and most of his men too. In fact all of 'em,' Nick added, thinking. 'One or two of them musta bin winged, but that didn't stop 'em escaping. We'd bin chasin' 'em from ranch to ranch, then we set about 'em as they came ridin' up the trail after settin' the town on fire here. We wasn't q;uick enough to stop 'em doing that.'

'What I don't get is: what's it all

about?' Dawlish demanded. 'What has Carterville, or the neighbouring ranchers, done to cause such a sudden and widespread onslaught? Has anybody any explanation to offer?'

'Just don't seem to be one,' Nick shrugged. 'I don't s'pose we'll be bothered with 'em again. Fur one thing they've done about all they can do, and for another they'll know every manjack'll be watchin' for 'em if they try again. As to who they are I ain't got the vaguest idea, nor have any of us.'

'A wandering band of outlaws is my guess,' Halligan commented, lounging forward. 'Fact remains there's bin one hell of a shindig tonight.'

'Yeah.' Nick aimed him a hard glance. 'Come to think on it, Halligan, I don't remember seein' you or your pardner here doin' very much when it came to the shootin'. You rode around plenty but sure did conserve on yuh ammunition.'

'I shot how and where I could,' Halligan retorted. 'Want to make somethin' of it?'

Nick looked for a moment as though he would have liked to have made plenty; then apparently he changed his mind.

'Those of our boys who wus finished we buried when the phantom and his men had ridden away,' he said. 'The sheriff's body is outside, tied to his horse. We reckoned that in his case there oughta be some sort of ceremony before we put him down.'

'You're right in that,' Dawlish acknowledged. 'Meantime the rest of us have got to consider how we stand. My partner here and I are willin' to do what we can to help. We're not regular inhabitants of Carterville but we're staying in the town indefinitely, so we — '

'You sure did plenty tonight, Mr Dawlish — and you, Mr Grant — in helping to put the fires out.'

It was an old-timer who spoke, coming forward as he did so. Then, as Dawlish had hoped, others took up the chorus.

'But for the way you got things

organized I guess everythin' might have been lost.'

'We're mighty grateful to you, gents.'

'Oh, come now . . . ' Dawlish gave his most magnanimous smile and looked about him. 'My partner and I simply saw the difficulty and helped you to straighten it out. And I still say we've got to decide what's to be done. Ranches have been destroyed, ranchers murdered, and many of you are without homes. We haven't even got a sheriff who can try and pick up the trail where the last one left off.'

'Shouldn't be difficult to get a new sheriff,' Halligan commented. 'Simply vote for it. All we want is nominations.'

'What about a mayor?' Dexter asked. 'Is there one in this town? I ain't ever seen one — '

'He was with the boys tonight,' Nick told him. 'He got rubbed out too. I reckon that this whole town of Carterville is like a ship without a rudder at the moment — an' that ain't good for any town. I don't see how we could do worse than nominate these two gents who've done such a lot to save the town tonight. Mr Dawlish for sheriff and Mr Grant for mayor.'

'Yeah, sure thing! That's a mighty good notion, Nick.'

'I second the nominations,' came Halligan's lazy voice.

'Okay then,' Nick said. 'We can take a hand vote. Those in favour of Mr Dawlish for sheriff raise their hands.'

From the look of things the vote was unanimous, chiefly no doubt because there just were no other men to stand in competition. Accordingly, in less than five minutes, Dawlish and Grant both found themselves elected to their respective offices. So far the tide was flowing entirely in Dawlish's direction and his beaming face was a clear guide to his feelings.

'All I can say is I much appreciate your trust in me and my friend, folks, and I can safely say we'll do all we can to justify it. It sorta gives us a good reason for staying in Carterville, too, instead of moving on.'

'Just what are you in Carterville for?' Halligan asked, rather surprisingly.

'Oh, just business.' Dawlish began fencing immediately. 'We have been considering the layout for making a new cattle centre here since we're both cattle men from the north. Nothing to stop us staying here, though, and fulfilling the offices you've given us. Eh, Grant?'

'Sure,' Grant acknowledged, somewhat quietly. He had his eyes on Halligan's hard face and piercing eyes. He wished he could do more to fathom what lay beyond that granite exterior and faintly contemptuous manner.

'Next thing to do is just a matter of formality,' Nick said. 'In the absence of a previous mayor we'll have to get the town lawyer to swear you in — then you're official.' He looked about him. 'Where's Mr Hennesy?'

Isaac Hennesy, the town's legal man, pushed himself forward and the situation was turned over to him. In consequence, in another fifteen minutes,

Dawlish and Grant found themselves legally vested with their respective authorities — Dawlish having obvious evidence in the shape of his star badge removed from the body of the former sheriff.

'Chasin' the hoodlums who caused tonight's trouble ain't going to be easy,' Nick said, when the formalities were over. 'I reckon no blame will attach to either of you gents if you never succeed in finding the outlaws. What we do look to you to do is get this town reorganized after the beatin' it's taken. That's always the job of mayor an' sheriff in a small township like this.'

'Rely on it,' Dawlish said, and Grant gave his usual nod of confirmation. 'Tomorrow we'll start out to see what we can do. Right now we drink — and everything's on me.'

Which move was sufficient to almost restore things to normal. Men and women broke up into groups and moved to either the tables or the bar. Dawlish drifted away thoughtfully, followed by Grant, then they brought up sharp as they found Halligan looming in front of them. That peculiar sardonic smile was twisting his big mouth.

'Congratulations,' he said laconically. 'I reckon the both of you have worked mighty hard for this — or so Nick's been telling me.'

'You'll all of you benefit,' Dawlish retorted. 'And if Nick has any sense he won't open his mouth too wide, or you either.'

Halligan shrugged. 'I know when I'm well off. Sure wouldn't do for the authorities to get wind of the fact that murder and arson have lifted you and Mr Grant to power.'

Dawlish and Grant glanced momentarily at each other.

'Say one word out of line, Halligan, and you're a dead man,' Dawlish said finally.

'Sure, sure. I'm not crazy. I just hope you don't take too long payin' up the balance of what you owe us fellers, that's all.'

With that he gave a nod and ambled

across to the bar. Dawlish tightened his lips and went on his way to the outdoors. In a moment Grant had joined him.

'Put it any way you like, Dawlish, I still don't like it.' Grant moodily surveyed the half wrecked town and the askew kerosene lamps. 'When trouble comes it'll be from Halligan. I wouldn't trust him any further than I could spit. Nick's crooked enough, but I'll gamble Halligan's worse.'

'Stop beefing, will you? Everything's under control and we've got the town in our hands.'

'For as long as we're willing to pay for the privilege, yes. But where's the money comin' from?'

'Control of the town also means control of its financial resources, such as they are. I'll figure out a wangle with the bank and get everything paid. Leave it to me. It won't be the first difficult money job I've tackled . . . Now let's get back to the hotel and work things out. In the morning we start business in earnest.'

3

It was only by slow degrees that the inhabitants of Carterville and the surrounding district began to realize that Dawlish and Grant were not quite so benevolent as they appeared to be. The first evidence of it appeared a week after they had assumed office and the town had been mainly restored to normal. Then it was that certain members of the town discovered that the solitary Carterville Bank had been taken over by the mayor. Just how the wangle had been brought about was not clear — so lawyer Isaac Hennesy suddenly found himself faced with a deputation demanding to know the facts. As the solitary legal expert nobody seemed better qualified than he to explain.

'Only way I can put it is to say that there's a state of emergency,' he said, leaning back in his swivel chair and closing one eye against the smoke of his cheroot. 'Like when there's a disaster anywheres the government declares martial law and takes over everythin'.'

'Mayor Grant ain't the government,' one of the deputation snapped. 'This sort of thing wants reportin' to Washington.'

'The mayor,' Hennesy said, with a placating smile, 'has not done anything crooked. You can rely on that. All he has done is marshal our financial resources into a common pool so that money can be wisely used for rebuilding damaged property and compensating the home-less ranchers, and others.'

This line of talk was straight up Hennesy's street, particularly so when he knew that his hearers were not particularly bright. As crooked as a snarled lariat himself, it had not been difficult for Dawlish to bribe him into spinning an apparently convincing line whilst finances were 'adjusted' to suit the circumstances.

'What rebuilding was necessary has bin done,' another man pointed out. 'As for compensation to the homeless ones, not a red cent has been handed out as yet.'

'We haven't got around to it. These things take time.'

'Look, Hennesy, quit stalling!' A big fellow with an angry face pushed forward. 'We go to the bank to draw some cash, and what do we get told? No withdrawals until the blasted mayor gives his permission! What kind of a racket do you call that? Much more of it and the boys'll be smashing the bank down and taking the law inter their own hands.'

'The mayor is absolute boss of the town,' Hennesy said, unshaken. 'He acts in conjunction with the sheriff and makes what regulations he thinks necessary to meet an emergency. He isn't doing anything crooked. In a day or two everything will be straight.'

The men and women looked at one another doubtfully, then finally one of them jerked his head and, flattened for the moment, the deputation left the office. Hennesy gave them reasonable time to break up and then he too got on the move. In a few minutes he had reached the sheriff's office where Dawlish and Grant had now made their headquarters. He found them in the midst of papers and deeds, working busily.

'Well, Hennesy?' Dawlish looked up briefly. 'What are you looking so damned cheerful about? And we're busy,' he added meaningly.

'I c'n see that,' the lawyer grunted. 'I thought it as well to give you warnin' that the townsfolk are getting restive about your ban on the bank. If it goes on much longer there'll be a flare-up and us three'll be in the centre of it.'

Dawlish gave a hard smile. 'Look, Hennesy, I'm not interested in the complaints of a lot of hayseeds. They'll do as they're told — and like it. The mayor here, at my order, has put this whole town under martial law following that attack, and the regulations that have been made won't be altered until things are straight. May not be for some time. There's a lot to do.'

'Such as?' Hennesy asked. 'Since I'm on the legal end of this I'd better know the facts.'

'No harm in you knowing some of 'em. Wouldn't do for you to have too much knowledge. You might get ideas. Firstly, we're taking over the Journey's End. That's the king-pin of the whole town and the main money-spinner.'

'Granted.' Hennesy sat down. 'How much are yuh payin' for it? Jed Grantham owns it.'

'I know; I have the deeds here. We've offered him — in the name of the Carterville Authority — our new title for civic control around here — the sum of five thousand dollars.'

Hennesy stared, even his grasping mind shaken for a moment.

'Five thousand? Why, it's worth twenty times that for the profit it makes.'

Dawlish grinned. 'Nobody's going to pay twenty times as much as they need, Hennesy. It works this way: the place has been badly wrecked, which knocks the value down. And secondly, Jed Grantham has a family he's crazy about.'

'Yeah, sure — wife and three daughters. What's that got to do with it?'

'We have no guarantee but what the phantom horseman and his outlaws may not return one night,' Dawlish said deliberately. 'I found out that Grantham is scared to all hell of that possibility, so I worked on it. I give him five thousand and full and constant protection for himself and his family against future attack. It doesn't mean a thing to me, or the men I'll put on guard, but it means everythin' in the world to Grantham. It's a matter of psychology, Hennesy — a matter of finding your man's weak spot and then concentrating everything upon it.'

'Uh-huh,' Hennesy admitted vaguely.

'Okay, if that's the way you've done it there ain't nothing I can do about it.'

'Nothing at all. You're a paid servant, and you'll continue to be well paid as long as you do as you're told. We're signing the deed with Grantham this afternoon. The other thing we're taking over is the General Stores. Half gutted after last night and at our estimate worth one thousand dollars. Kingsley, who runs it, thinks he's well off on that. His stock's gone, the place is in ruins, and nobody else would even make an offer. So that's another deed to be signed — and one of the main sources of revenue for the town. Like the Journey's End, it will come under the control of the Carterville Authority.'

'Which really means you and the mayor? You get the rake-off?'

'Since we do the thinking — or at least I do — we deserve the rake-off. We're using the town's money to make these two purchases and it'll be ploughed back out of the profits. All the bank is doing is lend us money to put the town back into working order. We know there will be dissenters, and there's only one way to treat 'em.'

'If you mean to use lead you've got the starting point of a war,' Hennesy said grimly, rising to his feet.

'Mebbe so.' Dawlish shrugged. 'Fact remains the town is in our hands and those who cause trouble must be put out of the way. Nick, Halligan, and one or two of the other boys, have all been told what to do. Control here, Hennesy, has to be absolute. Not only so's we can make money, but for other reasons as well.'

'I notice that yore mighty cagey about the 'other reasons'. If I'm supposed to handle the legal end of things I ought to know exactly what you aim to do.'

Dawlish hesitated for a moment, then looked down at the papers he and Grant had been studying. Now he came to notice, Hennesy saw that they were not entirely deeds but maps as well — big survey maps of the district for many miles around, most of the areas lined out in red ink.

'May as well tell him,' Grant said. 'He's bound to know soon anyhow.'

'Okay.' Dawlish looked directly at the waiting lawyer. 'The answer's a simple one, Hennesy — oil.'

Hennesy did not seem particularly moved by the statement. 'Oil, huh? I suppose you two know that you're about the fifth pair of prospectors who think they've found oil around here?'

'Meaning what?' Dawlish asked sourly. 'If there's been oil men before us why didn't they cash in on the fact? Or did they, like us, find the expense of buying out the landowners too much?'

'Nope, nothing like that. They simply found when they came to drill, that the oil didn't go deep enough to make it a working proposition, so they packed up and bothered no more.'

Grant looked startled. 'Say, Dawlish, do you suppose we've got things wrong? We made our tests with outdated instruments. Mebbe they made us more optimistic than we should've been.'

Dawlish, who had been studying Hennesy's face intently, shook his head.

'We didn't make any mistake, Grant. We've been in the game too long to do that — but I reckon it would suit friend Hennesy here if he could make us think we had. Wouldn't it, Hennesy?'

'Huh?' The lawyer looked flustered. 'How d'you mean?'

'You don't need telling!' Dawlish snapped. 'That was a twist I might have expected from you, Hennesy. If you could make us think we'd wasted our time in trying to find workable oil you'd have the whole thing for yourself. Right?'

'Not at all. I simply said that prospectors — '

'I know what you said — and don't try it again. We're here for oil and we mean to work it. Every man and woman will be at it within a month. Carterville will finally become one of the richest towns in the country, the centre of a mighty oil-bearing region.

You're a smart man, Hennesy, but not quite smart enough to cross me. Now get out. You know what we're working for and as I said before, you'll be well paid if you play the game straight. If you don't you can count yourself a dead pigeon.'

Hennesy said no more. He tightened his lips and went. The moment he had gone Grant turned sharply.

'Look, Dawlish, was he bluffing or not?'

'Of course he was. Wouldn't you if you could scare off two men from a fortune? Our tests are absolutely correct, and every one of these areas lined out in red are worth a fortune once we begin drilling. Anyway, the drilling comes later: we've first got to get control of the properties which can turn in money.'

And to this end Dawlish bent all his endeavours thereafter. That same day saw the signing of the two deeds which conveyed the Journey's End and the General Stores into Dawlish's waiting hands, after which he set to work to discover what other sources of revenue there might be. In the ensuing days he listed about half-a-dozen properties which would be useful, including the mail office-cum-grocery stores, then on the morning of the fourth day he was brought to a sudden cessation of his endeavours by the appearance of Halligan in the sheriff's office.

'Well, what do you want?' Dawlish demanded impatiently. 'Or can't you see I'm busy?'

'Sure I can see,' Halligan acknowledged, with his irritatingly calm voice. 'I figgered you must be so rapt up you even forgot to pay the men who worked for you. I'm here speakin' for 'em. Most of 'em, bar Nick, were kinda leary of tellin' you about it.'

'Nick is in charge,' Dawlish retorted. 'If there's anything to be said on behalf of the men it's for him to say it.'

'He would ha' done, only when it comes to it he's as scared of remindin' you of your obligations as the rest of

75

'em are. So I reckoned it was time I did something about it myself. You owe me five hundred dollars, Dawlish — and there are some eighteen other men who worked for nothing and nothing else but sweet promises who want a thousand dollars apiece for their night's work. I'm here to see that they get it.'

'They will, when I'm good and ready. Sums like that take time.'

'Not when you can buy the Journey's End and the General Stores with no more embarrassment than buying a two-bit cigar.'

'What the hell's that got to do with you?' Grant put in hotly. 'You've nothing to do with the financial control of this town, Halligan, and — '

'Financial control!' Halligan repeated scornfully. 'Dammit, gents, I wasn't born yesterday. All you two are doing is misappropriating the town's banking reserve so as to put yourselves in a position to wield absolute financial dictatorship. In a town of less dozey inhabitants than this you'd have been strung up for it long ago — But that's beside the point. All the boys have seen your financial juggling and their argument is that if you can do that you can pay them — and I agree with 'em.'

'I can't pay them until things turn round!' Dawlish thumped the desk.

'Sorry, Dawlish, but they're not prepared to wait for that, and neither am I. You'll pay them today or have a load of trouble on your hands.'

Dawlish's face hardened. 'I take it that all this is your own bright idea?'

'Sure thing.' Halligan gave his infuriating grin. 'I'm a man of action and I don't like to see the high-ups getting away with it while the ones taking the orders have to keep their mouths shut. Besides, I like being paid for what I do. I'm funny that way.'

'You will be paid,' Dawlish insisted. 'You don't seem to realize how many things I'm trying to sort out at once — '

'Frankly, I don't — and what's more I don't care. Just get the money paid by tonight or you're liable to lose a useful army of helpers and also have a lot of them opening their mouths too wide as to what you're up to.' Halligan's almost casual manner changed abruptly and his eyes narrowed to steely scrutiny. 'Get one thing straight, gentlemen. You've got away with murder, arson and misappropriation of town funds because nobody's spoken a word against you. That sort of monkey business needs paying for. You either pay up or by tomorrow morning the nearest authorities will have all the information laid in their laps and you two will be hitting leather in an effort to escape justice. Just think it over. No man, no matter how big, can trifle with me.'

Halligan turned and went and the door slammed. Grant scratched the back of his head and stood thinking — then after a moment Dawlish glared at him.

'Don't dare say it!' he almost snarled.
'What?'
'That this sort of thing is only to be

expected and — '

'Matter of fact I wasn't going to say anything of the kind. What I was wondering was: who the devil is this man Halligan and where does he come from? With Nick we had just the right man, but this critter seems to have taken the lead straight out of Nick's hands. As I said earlier he'll be the one we've got to reckon with before we're finished . . . better pay him and the rest of the boys up, then mebbe he and Dexter will leave town.'

'With so much to gain? I doubt it!' Dawlish stood and pondered for a while, his lips tight, then he gave a reluctant sigh. 'Just the same I agree with you that we've got to pay them off. We can't afford to have any of them against us. Going to be damned difficult to wangle things round, though.'

Difficult or otherwise Dawlish knew when he was cornered, so he spent the rest of the day working out how best to rob Peter and pay Paul. The result of his endeavours became clear that evening when, in the smoky noisiness of the Journey's End, he drifted to each of his men in turn and paid them up in greenbacks.

'Only one thing I ask,' he said, when he finally came to Nick, Halligan and Dexter standing together, 'and that is that you tip off the boys not to flourish their money all over the place. It might give the rest of the customers wrong ideas.'

'Rely on it,' Nick said promptly, in his most tractable mood with so much money in his pocket. 'I'll keep 'em good — and we'll also take care of anybody who starts a spiel against you.'

Dawlish nodded and returned to the midst of his customers. Some of them were friendly; some were not. He knew perfectly well that many townsfolk suspected him and Grant of wangling banking funds to their own advantage, but without any real proof nothing could be done. And, as Dawlish had calculated, men and women in this part of the world had to drink, and they had to pay for it. There lay the source of an income which would eventually straighten the warped finances of the Carterville Bank.

Altogether it took a month for things to turn round. In that time Dawlish and Grant established themselves completely. They paid most of the drifting menfolk a reasonable wage to get the town's principal buildings rebuilt, after which money came in from various sources — the saloon, the General Stores, and one or two other valuable holdings. There were no grumbles from the gunmen who kept the town in order. Indeed, the only dark spot was the constant presence of Halligan, usually contemptuously polite. It was evident he had not the least intention of departing. Possibly he had his own ideas on how much he might collect when the oil boom began.

And it was to the matter of oil that Dawlish at last turned his attention, but he was careful not to make any announcement concerning it until he had tipped Mayor Grant off to withdraw the restraint on the town's banking system. This was a good psychological stroke. It put the people in a more compromising mood and even got them around to thinking that perhaps Dawlish was not a crook after all but an organizing and financial genius.

Once he had assessed this move, Dawlish went into action. He called a meeting of the townsfolk in the Journey's End and with a good deal of back-patting for himself outlined his intention.

'I know full well that most of you, until recently, thought me one of the biggest crooks that had ever walked into Carterville,' he said, giving his disarmingly bland smile. 'And, believe me, it was tough for me to have to accept that suspicion. Since then I've proved you wrong. With Mr Grant's help as mayor I've restored the ruined parts of the town, balanced the bank's finances, paid many of you good wages to get things rebuilt, and generally done my best to act as a sheriff should. I even feel that if I asked for a vote of confidence from you I'd get it unanimously.'

'Sure thing,' somebody said promptly.

'Guess we had you figgered wrong, sheriff, but you know the way things looked.'

'There's one thing you haven't done, though,' Halligan remarked lazily, lounging against a nearby table.

'Well?' Dawlish's voice was acid. He felt himself bristling the moment Halligan spoke.

'You haven't found who the phantom rider is, or the men who worked with him. I know Nick here said you could be forgiven if you failed to discover any worthwhile evidences, but far as I can see you didn't even look. I think you should have, as sheriff of this territory.'

Dawlish gave him a grim look. 'When I took over as sheriff I had more pressing things to do in getting the town straight than in chasing rainbows.

I'd never have found anything, anyways.'

'How d'you know?' Halligan asked dryly. 'If you call murder and arson just chasin' rainbows then you've mighty queer ideas as a sheriff.'

'Aw, shut up, Halligan!' Nick said impatiently. 'The phantom rider and his boys got clean away with it, and I think the sheriff here acted in the only way he could at that time.'

'Well, I think he — '

'I said shut up!' Nick barked, glaring, and at that Halligan gave a faintly amused smile and shrugged his shoulders. To the rest of the men who had worked for Dawlish on the night of the attack it was a mystery why Halligan should want to drag up the affair anyway, since he had been mixed up in it. It was a mystery to Dawlish, too, and he moved fast to cover it up before the assembly could press the business too closely.

'I feel it is time I should reveal to you townsfolk that Mr Grant and I have made a discovery concerning this territory, of which Carterville is the centre — and it is that we're in the midst of oil.'

'Oil!' came a simultaneous shout, and for a moment every face was turned towards Dawlish, as he stood elevated on a chair beside the bar.

'It isn't guesswork,' he continued. 'Grant and I have been interested in oil for a number of years, even though we've never made much out of it — but recently, since being sheriff and mayor, we have come into possession of geological surveys. It was these that started us investigating. To cut a long story short we are in the midst of enormous wealth. It only needs drilling out of the earth.'

The clamour that broke forth prevented Dawlish from speaking for several minutes; then at last he raised a hand for silence.

'There are two possibilities ahead of us, my friends. One is that you trust me again to organize a labour team to drill for oil, along with the heavy financial demands which this will certainly make — or you can forget all about the business and have the pleasure of seeing other companies move into this region and work the oil for themselves. Either way let one thing be quite clear. I know there is oil, and I know where it is. It can make a fortune and I'd rather that fortune was received by you good people than by an independent company. If I can't get the labour and confidence here I'll go elsewhere, but that oil is going to be produced!'

Nick moved forward. 'Seems t'me there's no two ways about it, sheriff. Fur as I'm concerned I'd say you oughta go ahead and transform this town into an oil centre. Like you said, everyone is bound to benefit.'

'Sure! You do that, sheriff. If you do it as good as you've organized everythin' else we'll be on velvet.'

'How much finance will it take?' Halligan questioned, and Dawlish shrugged.

'That's not easy to say. It means the

transport and erection of oil derricks, cost of wages for labour, money again for transporting the oil to the nearest buyers — who'll most certainly be the North Texas Oil Company — '

'Have you contacted them yet?' asked lawyer Hennesy sharply. 'Or are you just assuming they'll be interested?'

'In business,' Dawlish answered coldly, 'it doesn't pay to assume anything. I know Dan Corton, the head of North Texas, as well as I know my partner Grant — and Corton will take all we can supply because their own yield isn't big enough to meet the demand. Later, mebbe, when we're fully established, we'll find other outlets at better prices, but that's in the dim future . . . But I was talking abut the expense. Those are the main items. If you folks are willing to trust me I can put Carterville and its environs on the map with a vengeance. It can become one of the richest townships that ever was.'

'I don't see why we can't form a Corporation,' Hennesy remarked. 'Let the townsfolk be the shareholders. Let them put in what money they feel they can afford.'

'No use whatever,' Dawlish answered brusquely. 'It would never amount to enough. It will take every cent this town's got to get things launched, and the only way to handle it is for me to control the money unquestioned. Needless to say it will repay itself a thousand times over the moment oil appears.'

'Which,' Halligan pointed out, 'puts you and Grant in a position to take the full rake-off, and you won't be answerable to anybody.'

'In the absence of a recognized company, yes,' Dawlish retorted, 'but naturally a statement of expenditure and profit will be issued from time to time. Mr Hennesy will see to that, won't you?'

'Yeah,' the lawyer assented, realizing there was nothing else he could do but agree.

'Very well then, that's it,' Dawlish said, spreading his hands. 'Have I your agreement to carry on, or not?'

'Take a vote on it,' Nick suggested. 'Everybody in favour of supporting Mr Dawlish and the mayor raise their hands.'

The hands rose instantly, and the only dissenter was Halligan. He kept his hands in his pockets and surveyed the scene impassively. Dawlish gave him a grim look.

'I take it I haven't your support, Halligan?'

'Right; you haven't. The only thing I'd be in favour of is a Corporation, properly organized and managed. However, since I'm in the minority my opinion doesn't count anyway.'

'You're damned right it doesn't,' Nick confirmed. 'You've got a habit of always wantin' everythin' different to everybody else, Halligan, and one day that's goin' to get you in bad with the rest of us. Meantime, Mr Dawlish, we're solidly behind you.'

Dawlish smiled and said no more. He had won his point and the way was wide open . . .

★ ★ ★

Dawlish wasted no more time. With absolute carte blanche to do as he chose he went the whole hog, commencing with ordering the necessary materials for oil derricks from the East Texas Timber Company. To give the orders was one thing, but to devise a means of transport was another. As far as Carterville itself was concerned nothing more ambitious than buckboards could be provided, entirely inadequate for the desert and mountain trail which would have to be followed. The heavy load alone would probably smash the buckboards in pieces.

So Dawlish went to work on another angle. He rode out specially to the East Texas Timber Company, studying the route as he went, and the outcome of his talks with the company finally produced a giant wagon which, with six horses, would be loaned for a concession. Dawlish did not like the extra money which was needed but he had no choice other than to pay for it.

Upon his return to Carterville he immediately sent for Halligan and Nick. They arrived promptly enough in the sheriff's office, both of them wondering what new move was afoot.

'What do you two boys know about heavy freight-wagon driving?' Dawlish asked briefly.

'I can handle it,' Halligan responded, with his usual supercilious self-assurance.

'Don't worry me none,' Nick said, shrugging. 'What's the angle, boss?'

'Just this. There are three loads of derrick timber to be brought from the East Texas Timber Company. They can provide their own drivers and rocket the price — or I can provide my own and they'll supply the wagon and team. If you think you can handle it between you the job's yours. It'll be one hell of a trip: I've made it already on horseback. Bad mountain passes to the east, and a good deal of soft desert trail afterwards.'

'Nothing in that scares me,' Halligan

said. 'Naturally we'll be well paid for it?'

Dawlish gave a hard smile. 'Never forget that angle, Halligan, do you?'

'I guess not. I never could see the point of workin' for nothin'. I'd say two hundred dollars for both-way ride — every time we do it — would be reasonable.'

'You'll take a hundred and fifty,' Dawlish snapped. 'Each of you.'

Halligan turned. 'Okay. Nick may be crazy enough to take that figure but I won't. See you again, boss — '

'Wait — wait!' Dawlish gave a sigh and tightened his lips. 'You know damned well there are no two other men I can rely on like you two for a tough job like this — '

'Check,' Halligan grinned. 'That's why you've got the pleasure of paying for it. I'll take half of mine now and then I'm ready to go the moment you say so.'

Dawlish did not argue any further. His face grim he opened a steel cash-box and handed over half-payment to each man.

'Get going as soon as you can,' he ordered. 'The minute we get that first consignment the rest of the boys can start on the derricks. We've got the oil-bearing areas cleared so there won't be any delay in that direction. On your way.'

Halligan and Nick both departed promptly, then after musing bitterly for a moment or two upon the money-grabbing tactics of the men who worked for him Dawlish turned his attention to other matters. There were many things to do now his plans were really maturing. There was the matter of ordering oil-drilling equipment, for instance, the vital materials necessary to draw the precious fluid from the earth.

And, meanwhile, Nick and Halligan set out on the long horse-ride to eastern Texas. They realized by the time the trip was over — a good eight hours' gruelling ride — that Dawlish had not been exaggerating when he had referred to the rigours of the trip. It would take every ounce of horsemanship and nerve to negotiate some of the mountain passes — particularly one S-bend where there was on one side a drop of a thousand feet to a ravine below; and the desert sand would doubtless provide many a problem too if the wagon once drifted from the main trail. However, neither man was dismayed. Whatever else they might be they were neither of them lacking in courage and resource.

The East Texas Timber Company was located a couple of miles from the town of Sarcot's Bend, and it was in this town that the two men decided to pass the night. Inevitably they drifted to the town's main saloon and, to Nick at least, this seemed as good an opportunity as any to try and penetrate the iron reserve of Halligan and get to know more about him. Away from the environment of Carterville, and his partner Dexter, it might be possible to learn more about the man. Deep down Nick had a profound distrust of him, and he wanted to know why.

Within the first half-hour of their being seated at a corner table Nick knew he was flogging a dead horse. Halligan remained as much on the defensive as ever, usually ignoring most of the questions aimed at him, or else smiling cynically. To make even a scratch on the granite was impossible.

'Well . . . ' Nick drained the last of his whisky. 'I s'pose the best thing we can do is get a good rest before tomorrow. If we start at sunup we should make the trip in a day.'

'Yeah,' Halligan acknowledged. 'I reckon we — '

He paused abruptly, so abruptly that Nick glanced at him in surprise. It was unusual to see a look of consternation on Halligan's face, but it was certainly there now. He was staring fixedly at a big man in a black suit and Stetson hat who had just entered through the batwings and was lounging across the bar.

'Okay, let's go,' Halligan said, recovering himself suddenly.

'Sure.' Nick eyed him, then the newcomer, and got to his feet. Halligan moved with uncommon speed between the tables towards the batwings, but before he had completed the trip a powerful bass voice hailed him:

'Well, if it isn't Dick Charters!'

Halligan stopped and so did Nick. Halligan turned slowly, plainly making an effort to keep a grip of himself. The big man in the black suit had come forward from the bar, his hand extended.

'Last man in the world I expected to see around here, Dick! Come and have a drink and tell me how you're getting on.'

'Eh? Oh, yes — sure thing.' It was odd to see the cocksure Halligan at a loss. 'I've a partner here — Nick.'

Nick moved forward and the next thing he knew his hand had been seized in a crushing grip.

'Right glad to know you,' the big fellow smiled. 'Spencer's the name — Cameron Spencer of the North

Texas Oil Company. Dan Corton and I run the company between us.'

Dan Corton? Salthouse remembered something vaguely — Why yes, Dawlish had referred to the name when explaining his plans to the people of Carterville.

'Nick's working with me for Dawlish,' Halligan hurried on. 'So he — '

'Knows everything about everything, eh?' Spencer boomed. 'That's fine! Saves the hell of a lot of secrecy. Here, what'll be your pleasure, boys?'

They had reached a table and Nick promptly asked for the inevitable whisky. Halligan muttered something about rye, his brow furrowed and trouble staring out of his eyes. Not that this seemed to affect the booming man-mountain Spencer. He got the drinks himself from the barkeep and then lumbered over to the table.

'Don't get the wrong angle when I say Nick's with me for Dawlish,' Halligan said, almost desperately. 'What I mean is, we're both on Dawlish's payroll.'

Spencer looked as if he were puzzling things out for a moment, then he shrugged wide shoulders.

'Nice to know two of you are working on it anyway. How's about Dexter? He still pulling along?'

'Sure — sure. He's with us, too.'

'Swell!' Spencer took a long drink and then blew out his cheeks expressively. 'Had a damned thirsty ride today. No small hop from the company to here. Had to come, though. Special business to see to at the bank . . . Well, Charters, how's things coming along at your end?'

Halligan did not answer. He gave Nick a covert glance, and met one of profound mystification in return. Nick's struggle at the moment was to decide why Halligan had suddenly become 'Charters', and also where Spencer fitted into the problem.

'Quite all right,' Halligan — 'Charters' — answered tamely.

'Quite all right? But darn it, man, that doesn't convey anything! Why can't you be more explicit? Since we've happened to meet you may as well tell me everything and save sending in a long report.'

Halligan ignored the fact that Nick was watching him intently and made a fierce silencing grimace. Spencer saw it, and a light seemed to dawn.

'Oh! Confidential, huh?'

'Naturally!' Halligan retorted fiercely. 'Say much more and you're likely to gum up the whole works! I'll report in the normal way soon as I can. Now I've got to be going. Coming, Nick?'

'Sure,' Nick agreed vaguely, rising — and Spencer looked from one to the other.

'Can't you even tell me what you're doing in Sarcot's Bend?' he demanded. 'You're ways off your territory.'

'Business,' Halligan told him shortly. 'I'll be in touch later . . . '

He jerked his head and Nick followed him through the batwings to the outdoors. There was silence between them for a while as they walked across the main street to their hotel, then presently Halligan gave a glance.

'I s'pose you're wondering what in heck all that was about?'

'Wouldn't you?' Nick countered.

'Ain't nothing really,' Halligan said, without much conviction. 'As he said, Spencer's one of the top men with North Texas Oil — a blabbermouth if ever there was one. I usta work for them once under the phony name of Charters. I wasn't exactly fired, but Spencer sent me on a special mission of his own which I never completed. That was what he was referring to tonight. Dexter was in on it with me. I suppose,' Halligan finished, as they mounted the steps of the hotel, 'Dexter and me will have to finish the job Spencer assigned us, otherwise he might make trouble.'

'Uh-huh,' Nick agreed, lost in thought. Indeed he did not quite know what to think yet, but of one thing he was reasonably sure. Not one word of what Halligan had said had the slightest ring of truth about it.

4

Nick was one of the last men in the world to be afflicted with sleeplessness, but on this particular occasion repose just would not come. He lay awake in his hotel room, thinking, turning matters over in his mind, pondering on all that Halligan — alias Charters — had said, and particularly the statements of Spencer.

Prolonged thinking was also uncommon with Nick, but on this occasion the mystery of Halligan absorbed him since he was desperately anxious to sort out the man's character, mainly to discover if he might not represent a threat in the future to Nick's so far unchallenged leadership of the Carterville gunmen.

Most of the night passed for Nick as he sifted the details, then just as he felt he had the right answer he fell asleep, and did not wake again until he heard somebody banging on the bedroom door.

'Get a move on, Nick. Be sunup in half-an-hour.'

'Okay,' Nick mumbled, and began to bestir himself. And, as he dressed and shaved, his meditations of the night came back to him, and with it the sureness that his conclusions were correct. If so, the sooner he got at the truth the better, and there'd be plenty of time for that during the ride back to Carterville.

Whilst breakfast was eaten he said little, and made no reference whatsoever to Spencer and the previous night's incidents in the saloon; then he and Halligan paid their bill and set off for the timber company, entering the great loading yard as the first gash of intense sunlight was breaking the eastern sky.

They stabled their horses with the company, with whom they would remain until the last journey home, and then took their first look at the wagon load of timber they were to drive back to Carterville. Neither of them said anything even though both were somewhat taken aback by the enormous size of the wagon and the amount of derrick timber packed upon it. Definitely it would need all their skill and the strength of the six powerful horses to land the consignment at its destination.

'Ready?' Halligan asked, as brusque as ever.

'Sure,' Nick acknowledged, and climbed up beside him.

They paused only long enough to make a check of their food and water supply, including fodder and water barrels for the horses, then Halligan released the brake and snapped the reins sharply on his own three horses. Nick followed suit and the great wagon began to move out of the yard in a cloud of dust and presently gained the main trail which, two miles further on, made connection with the treacherous mountain declivities leading down to the desert.

'You don't seem to have much to say for yourself this morning, Nick,' Halligan commented, as they drove on steadily into the glare of the morning. 'Something eating you?'

'Nope. Just didn't have much of a night. Room too hot mebbe.'

Halligan shrugged and made no comment. Neither did Nick speak again. He was still chewing over his thoughts of the night before, and he still believed the conclusion he had come to was the right one. If so, the sooner he had it out the better. It was not part of Nick's nature to suppress anything for long. He was always a man of action.

The bumping wagon and snorting horses had reached the first of the mountain trails before Nick had worked out what he intended to say. Then:

'How long have yuh bin working for North Texas Oil, Halligan?'

'Huh?' Halligan gave a surprised glance, busy with his horses. 'I worked for them a while back, like I told you.'

'I don't mean that — an' I don't believe it. I mean how long have you bin working for them? According to my reckonin' that's what you're still doing.'

'Then you're reckoning's screwy. I work for Dawlish, same as you.'

'Sure you do? Sometimes a guy can work for two people at once, if it suits his pocket. And, loco though I may be, that's what I think you're doin' and have been doin' for some time.'

Halligan's jaw set suddenly. He grasped the brakehandle with savage force and dragged it up. With a grinding of wheels the wagon came to a halt, the horses whinnying in protest at the too-sudden stop.

'Now, what the hell are you talkin' about?' Halligan demanded, his right hand gun abruptly jumping into his hand. 'Let your hair down, Nick, and say what you mean.'

'It's simple enough.' Nick kept a wary eye on the gun. 'I guess I don't pretend to be very bright, but this time

I'm sure I've got it straight. It's the only way to explain lots of the things you've done, to say nothin' of explainin' the cagey way you behave. You joined in with us in destroyin' the ranches, an' helped in lots of other ways, and tried to get guilt on Dawlish on several occasions. You tried to get him nailed for monkeyin' around with town funds: that's only one of the things you did. And I reckon the reason for all that is 'cos North Texas Oil wanted it that way. Even I can see that with Dawlish outa the way there'd be nothing to stop North Texas stepping in. You've got as much pull with the boys of Carterville as I have, so you could soon rub me out and take over.'

'Figgered quite a lot, haven't you, for a man with a pigeon-sized brain?' There was an ugly glint in Jim Halligan's eyes.

'The way you say that makes me believe I'm right. Yore working for North Texas, along with that partner of yours Dexter, an' you've both bin at it all along. Your aim, I reckon, is to get

106

rid of Dawlish, Grant, an' the rest of 'em as easily as possible without attractin' guilt to yourself — then Texas can step in.'

'I'll never know how you hit on the answer,' Halligan said slowly, 'but you're right. Quite right.'

'An' you sit there and admit it?' Nick stared in amazement.

'Sure thing. I'd gain nothin' by denying it. I am working for North Texas, and my orders is to sabotage everythin' Dawlish tries to do — even wipe him out by 'accident' if a good opportunity arises. I'll tell you this much, Nick — Texas can be trusted to pay up and keep their promises. Dawlish fur his part I wouldn't trust a coupla yards. Sooner or later set-backs are goin' to drive Dawlish outa business — even outa the territory altogether. If you've any sense you'll climb on the bandwagon along with me and later you'll be a top man with Texas, same as I will. Naturally I wouldn't ha' told you any of this if Spencer hadn't got the wrong angle and opened his mouth too wide.'

Nick sat thinking. Out of the corner of his eye he saw Halligan's gun-hand droop slowly as he relaxed.

'I ain't what you can call a man of scruples,' Nick said at length. 'I'll always work fur the best opportunity an' I wouldn't hesitate at rubbing a man out if I thought he wus in the way of what I wanted to do. But I reckon I've a certain sense of loyalty even to Dawlish though I don't trust him. One thing I've no time for, an' that's a two-timer.'

'Meaning what?' Halligan asked deliberately, his face taut.

'Meaning — this!' Suddenly Nick lunged. His right hand shot out and gripped Halligan's gun wrist. He twisted with all the strength he possessed but Halligan had more strength than Nick had reckoned. He resisted the tremendous pressure and, by straining every muscle, brought the gun slowly round.

Nick swore, his face a sweating mask of strain. With a final effort he deflected the gun at the instant Halligan fired it — but the noise of the shot had unpredictable results. In the confined area of these mountains the explosion of the gun was deafening. The horses reared and lunged with fright.

'Take it easy, you damned fool!' Halligan yelled. 'If these blasted horses once — '

Nick was not listening. He slammed out his left fist with devastating impact, knocking Halligan backwards on the box seat. He made a desperate effort to save himself flying over the edge of the truck but by sheer misfortune he grabbed the brake rod. The plunging horses, finding no resistance, started stumbling forward, snorting and whinnying. Nick did not even seem to notice that the wagon was on the move along the dangerously narrow trail. All he knew was that he had always hated the sneering Halligan and to know that he was also running with the hare and the hounds had proven the last straw. Nick, for all his villainous nature, had a curious streak of loyalty. He had never been known to let down a colleague or a boss, even though they might be as crooked as himself.

So he hammered and smashed his fists into Halligan without mercy, never giving him a chance to recover. His gun dropped at length and he tried to lash out and protect himself.

For such a battle on the driving-seat there could only be one end, with the horses in their frightened condition. They kept on plunging ahead frantically, the great wagon rumbling and bumping over the rocks and loose stones ... then came that deadly S-bend which curved around the thousand-foot ravine. Nick and Halligan both saw what was coming and stopped in their struggles, staring in fatal fascination.

They had time to notice the edge of the narrow trail sweeping towards them, then their whole universe was a tumbling riot of mountains and falling timber as they were flung out into space over the abyss. Screaming, they dropped helplessly, wagon and horses and timber smashing down the rock faces in an avalanche. Within seconds there was only a rising cloud of dust to show what had happened.

But from some distance back along the trail a lone rider had seen it all. He and his horse remained motionless until the dust had dispersed, then he turned and rode away.

★   ★   ★

That same evening in the Journey's End Dawlish was commencing to feel worried. It was more than time for the wagon and its load of derrick timber to have arrived, even allowing for the inevitable delays of such a journey.

'It's got me worried,' he confessed to Grant, as they both sat at a table near the bar and drank at intervals. 'They'd leave around sun-up and even allowing for everything else that ought to have brought them here by now.'

Grant shrugged. 'They'll get here, sooner or later. There aren't any tricks they can get up to with a load of timber as big as that — and besides they'll want to claim the rest of their money.'

'Yeah, I guess you're — '

Dawlish broke off and jumped in sudden alarm at a splintering crash from the big window not far behind him. Customers twirled round; men at the bar straightened up and instinctively dropped their hands to their guns. For a moment it seemed as though somebody had fired a bullet from the outside — then a cowpoke moved forward and picked up a piece of paper rolled around a chunk of stone. He stood frowning at it.

'Fur you, sheriff,' he said finally, and handed it over.

Grim-faced, Dawlish got to his feet and caught the missive as it was tossed to him, but before he could unravel it two men came blundering in through the batwings, their eyes popping.

'It's the phantom agen!' one of 'em gasped, swinging an arm backwards to indicate the street. 'We just see'd him riding through — the both of us.'

The second man nodded urgently and then hurried across to the bar for a drink.

'The phantom?' Grant repeated, astonished. 'You sure?'

He knew as well as Dawlish that since Nick had been the original phantom horseman it was beyond reason that there could be a second one.

'Sure I'm sure,' retorted the cowpoke who had broken the news. 'Mebbe another attack comin' up; I wouldn't know. We see'd him ridin' through the main street an' — '

'Shut up a minute,' Dawlish ordered curtly. 'Listen to this!'

By this time he had straightened out the note and tossed the chunk of stone on the table. He read deliberately.

' 'Your load of timber is at the bottom

of a ravine two miles south of Sarcot's Bend. Horses, wagon and your two drivers are also in the ravine. That is the first reply from the Phantom Avenger'.'

There was a stunned silence for a moment or two, everybody staring at Dawlish as he gazed in mystification straight ahead of him.

'But — but how the devil can it be the Phantom?' Grant asked at last. 'He's — '

'Shut up!' Dawlish ordered flatly, glaring at him, and realizing he had been on the very edge of a decidedly unguarded statement. Grant subsided. Dawlish balled the note up in his hand and looked about him.

'Apparently,' he said bitterly, 'we still haven't finished with the phantom rider who destroyed half of this town. The two drivers referred to are — or were — Nick and Halligan.' Dawlish found himself aware of a certain relief amidst this confusion. For an unknown phantom to be operating outside his sphere of influence created the impression that he — Dawlish — had no possible connection with the business, which in truth he had not on this occasion.

'If we've lost all that derrick timber we're in one hell of a mess,' Grant exclaimed.

'And Nick and Halligan too!' Dexter added grimly. 'If they've been killed it's just plain murder. Hey, you!' He looked at the cowpoke who had burst in with the news that he had seen the phantom rider. 'You say you saw the Phantom. Which way was he going?'

'North,' the cowpoke answered promptly, and his colleague gave a quick nod of confirmation.

'Only one thing for it, Sheriff,' Dexter said. 'We'll head north as well and see if we can find him.'

'I'm all for it,' Dawlish agreed, 'but there are two matters that need attention. On the one hand we've got to try and find the Phantom: on the other a party of us have got to ride out as fast as possible to this ravine near Sarcot's Bend and see what's happened. Best thing we can do is split in half in this emergency. You, Grant, are my deputy: lead the party in the search for the Phantom and take a dozen men with you. The rest of you will ride with me to the mountains . . . Let's go.'

There was no further hesitation. Men hurried immediately for the batwings, Dawlish, Grant and Dexter in the forefront. In a matter of minutes provisions and ammunition had been gathered and — for Dawlish's party — an extra supply of ropes and medical necessities. Then the journey began . . . Not very long afterwards Grant and his men started off too, not with much hope, however. To locate the phantom rider in the dark would probably prove an impossible feat.

Dawlish, for his part, did a good deal of hard thinking as he rode onwards. For the life of him he could not understand what had happened. Nick was the only 'phantom' he had ever known, so this newcomer was a mystery — and apparently a dangerous one. If he was able to strike with such vicious certainty as this the future was dubious indeed.

Inevitably, as the ride continued and the hours wore on, the first energies of the party began to flag, and so did the strength of the horses. Stops were made for rest under the stars and rising moonlight; then on again, mile after mile, until sheer exhaustion demanded sleep.

'We're not supermen,' Dawlish announced, as they drew to a halt at his orders, 'and there's a limit to what horse-flesh can stand. We'll stay here for the night and sleep, then carry on at down. A few hours can't make much difference anyways.'

So it was decided. Bed-rolls were unfastened and provisions unloaded. After a brief supper, after which the horses were fed, watered, and blanketed against the chill of the night, the men prepared for sleep — awakening again as the desert mists began to roll away before the first beams of the morning sun.

Breakfast — and then on again. This time with renewed energy as the first glimpse of the mountains of Sarcot Bend became visible as a purple blur on the horizon ... More hours, endless riding as it seemed, the sun rising up to hurl forth its torrid blaze on the grim-faced, sweating men and steaming horses.

So, after a stop for a mid-day meal, the trail leading from desert to mountains was at last reached. Dawlish, in the forefront, turned and looked back at his followers.

'This is the only possible trail there is from Sarcot's Bend, boys, so keep your eyes open. I've covered this route before, remember, so I know what I'm talking about.'

He whipped his horse on again, following thereafter the narrow, dangerous track which led through the foothills. In half-an-hour the weary, foam-flecked horses had reached the S-bend and Dawlish drew to a halt with a sudden jerk. He did not need to say anything: the rest of the men saw the scene below at the same time.

Far down, almost remote, were the smashed remains of the timber wagon, the timber itself thrown clear and lying like a multitude of scattered matchsticks. Apparently the wagon had struck a ledge and there splintered to pieces. Beyond the ledge was the ravine proper, an area of grey, merciless rock picked out here and there with vaguely discernible shapes.

Dawlish pulled a pair of powerful, city-made field-glasses from his kit and focussed them quickly. After a moment he gave a long, low whistle.

'Two bodies down there — evidently Halligan and Nick,' he said. 'I can also see two dead horses: the others must have slipped lower out of sight.'

'Better go down and see,' Dexter said promptly, dismounting, but Dawlish lowered the glasses and shook his head.

'No point in doing that, Dexter. Those bodies are more'n a thousand feet down and we couldn't do anythin' even if we could get at 'em. Our worry is the timber. We've got to have it, and a fresh wagon and team.'

'And leave Halligan and Nick there?' one of the men asked.

'Why not?' Dawlish shrugged. 'Waste of time pulling up corpses, besides the danger to ourselves. Nope: we concentrate on the timber. Get the ropes. We'll go down and weigh up the situation.'

The men dismounted and the various ropes were brought into use. To descend to the higher level, where the wagon had dropped, was not too difficult even though it was a dizzying job. Dawlish, Dexter, and one or two of the other men descended. The others remained above for orders.

'Nothing else for it but to get a mobile crane from the timber company,' Dawlish said at length, after the survey of the chaos was complete. 'Load it on to another wagon. Going to cost plenty, but cheaper than getting another lot of timber and leaving this here. When I get my hands on that

Phantom,' he finished, clenching his fists, 'I'll put every bullet I've got straight through him. Just how he contrived a smash like this I don't know but he sure did it properly. Okay, let's get back above.'

Back on the trail once more Dawlish made his decision known and then set off personally for the Timber Company, knowing full well he was the only man who would be able to get any worthwhile action. And even he had to use all his persuasion. The company was not at all anxious to permit the use of a mobile crane on such a dangerous part of the mountains, but at length Dawlish had his way even though the estimate of the cost — to say nothing of the charge for a new wagon and team and loss of the previous one and horses — shook him considerably.

In any case this was no time to be assessing costs. The situation had to be put straight first, then he could figure things out afterwards. So he went ahead of the crane and wagon to direct the route and by mid-afternoon the work of salvaging had commenced. Thanks to the crane, precariously balanced, the job was not a long one. The timber was hoisted up and laid in the nearby emergency wagon, the work finally being completed as the sun was sliding down behind the mountain tops.

'Yeah, that about does it,' Dawlish said, surveying the area from which the timber had been cleared. Then he looked beyond into the ravine's depths for a final study of the bodies of horses and men — but they had disappeared in the evening fog already rolling up from the depths.

'You're okay from here, Mr Dawlish?' the crane-driver called, and Dawlish turned and nodded.

'Sure thing. We'll drive the wagon ourselves. Thanks for the help.'

The crane began to move slowly backwards along the difficult trail and Dawlish began the job of rounding up his men and making sure the timber was secure upon the wagon for the rough ride back to Carterville. This done he signalled Dexter to be his co-driver and then took up the reins.

The wagon began moving, watched with breathless intentness by the men to the rear. Once or twice the wagon wheels came close to the edge of the narrow track and then swerved back to the centre. So, by degrees, the wagon progressed — and nobody breathed heavier sighs of relief than Dawlish and Dexter when at last the worst part of the trail had been negotiated and they had the clear trip through the foothills to the desert trail before them.

Once upon the desert itself they stopped for a meal and a much-needed rest, a process they repeated several times on the journey home, mainly because of the heavy load the wagon horses had to pull. Only when the halfway mark had been reached did they pause and decide to spend the night . . .

And it was whilst Dawlish and his

men were slogging their timber load across the desert that other things, less spectacular but just as significant, were taking place in Carterville. For, just after sundown, when the kerosene street lights had been burning for only ten minutes, a lone white figure rode silently into town from the north, sat well astride a perfectly white horse. Nobody saw him arrive. He had chosen that moment between the end of the day's work and the beginning of the trek to the saloon — that hour when most of the small populace was having an evening meal.

One man, though, had not gone home as yet, and apparently the lone rider was well aware of it. He rode his white horse round the back of the buildings and finally alighted at the rear of the small wooden edifice where Hennesy, the lawyer, had his offices. That the lawyer was still at work was amply proclaimed by the oil lighting visible through the front windows.

Actually he was working late on

various legal documents, most of them connected with Dawlish and his 'wangling' of land and money, a task he found so absorbing he did not even hear the Phantom's silent entry by the back regions.

For a moment the Phantom stood looking into the office through a crack of the door which led into the tiny kitchen regions; then he drew up his white neckerchief over his mouth and nose, took out his .45, and entered into Hennesy's presence.

The lawyer glanced up once from his work at the slight sounds, and then resumed his job — only to look up again with a violent start as he realized what had diverted his attention. Fixedly he stared at the white figure which had now come into the full range of the brightly burning desk lamp.

'Who — who the hell are you?' Hennesy whispered, his forehead suddenly gleaming.

'That's a pretty idiotic question, Hennesy,' the masked figure replied.

'You know perfectly well that I'm the Phantom Avenger, and I'm here because you're next on my list. The list is a fairly long one, incidentally, and each name on it has to have a line through it before I'm finished.'

Hennesy made a hard effort to recover himself. He sat forward in his swivel chair, trying to penetrate the disguise of the face kerchief, or else identify the voice. In both endeavours he failed lamentably.

'Thanks for deciding to work late,' the Phantom continued. 'Saves me a good deal of time — '

'You can't have anything to do with me — at least nothing to avenge,' Hennesy protested. 'I've had no dealings with the Phantom Horseman. I haven't even tried to locate him, like lots of the other men in this town.'

'Depends which Phantom you're talking about, Hennesy. The first one ranged up a lot of hoodlums behind him and destroyed every ranch in sight, killing most of the occupants. He also devised a destructive terror-raid on this town. That particular phantom rider has already been dealt with. Since phantoms seem to be in fashion I've turned into one too, only I'm an avenger. My sole object is to hand back to the culprits the death and misery they have handed out to others — '

'Well you can't include me in that! I haven't done anything to anybody.'

'Not in physical violence perhaps, but you have done a lot of legal swindling in order to help Dawlish to get the land he wants, to say nothing of various properties. I'm wise to you, Hennesy: I know exactly what you've been up to . . . ' The Phantom chuckled behind the kerchief. 'So you wonder how I know? I'll tell you. I've been here one or two nights and had a look at the work on which you've been engaged. You're rotten all through, Hennesy, like the rest of the corrupt gang trying to run this town.'

Hennesy breathed hard, gripping the arms of his chair. Then he suddenly burst out into another defensive argument.

'Listen — whoever you are! Everything I've done has been under orders from Dawlish. I don't even approve of one half of the things he's doing, but I've no choice but to obey him.'

'No? A man needs to be answerable to only one thing, Hennesy — his conscience. Since you haven't even made any attempt to stand out against Dawlish's demands on you it's pretty plain that you are as crooked as he is. Therefore you'll have to go the same way.'

Hennesy knew in that moment that he was finished if he did not act with devastating speed. Even as the realization dawned upon him his hand dropped to his gun, but he never had the chance to draw it. The Phantom leapt forward, tossing his own gun to the desk as he did so. With powerful hands he seized both of the scrawny lawyer's wrists and dragged them behind his back. Before he could do a thing Hennesy found his hands securely pinned behind him; then he was hauled to his feet by the Phantom's grip on his coat lapels.

'You're an easy one to deal with, I guess,' the Phantom murmured, and for a moment Hennesy thought he saw the glint of cold grey eyes above the mask. 'Not much of you. Be a tougher job to deal with Dawlish, or Grant.'

'For God's sake why don't you listen?' Hennesy panted. 'I ain't got nothing to do with — '

The Phantom took no notice. Deliberately he took from his hip-pocket a length of thin, strong rope, obviously placed there for exactly this purpose. Hennesy watched, his eyes staring in fright, and at the same time he tried to dislodge his bound wrists from the thin, cutting twine which held them. Quite without avail.

Then the Phantom moved, and the lawyer watched in stunned fascination as he saw the thin rope being fastened securely to the ceiling beam, whilst a sliding noose was carefully fashioned at the other end of the rope.

'Now ... ' The Phantom came forward. 'What I am doing is just, Hennesy — just insofar that you're mixed up with the gang who don't stop at the slaughter of the innocents just as long as they can gain their own ends. For scum of that type there's only one answer.'

Hennesy opened his mouth to give a mighty yell for help, but instead he found his own neckerchief thrust into it. Before he could spit the gag out deed-sealing tape was plastered to either side of his mouth, holding the gag in place.

The Phantom's next moves were simple but ruthlessly efficient. He lifted up Hennesy's struggling form in his powerful arms and thrust his head through the dangling noose of the rope. Then he took away his support. It was as simple as that. He did not even look at the choking man though he was compelled to hear his anguished gasps and strangled cries as he fought for the breath which had been cut off from his lungs.

Throughout Hennesy's death struggles the Phantom methodically printed a brief message on one of Hennesy's own memorandum sheets. This message he pinned to the dead Hennesy's chest and then left as silently as he had come, leaving the silhouette of the dangling body clearly visible on the wall as the oil lamp cast its radiance . . . And in ten minutes the Phantom had completely left town and vanished in the night.

It was an hour later when Hennesy was discovered by his wife, and it would not have happened even then had she not begun to wonder why he had not come home in the usual way. In the space of fifteen minutes the whole town knew about it, including Mayor Grant and his men, still smarting from their unsuccessful efforts to find the Phantom the night before. Upon Grant, as deputy sheriff, there now descended the full onus of responsibility until Dawlish returned.

But Grant knew full well, with a chill at his heart, that any effort he might again make to find the Phantom would only end in failure. The note pinned to the corpse of Hennesy was straight to the point:

SO MY LIST WILL BECOME SHORTER! DAWLISH, GRANT, DEXTER — YOU ARE ALL MARKED MEN. SOMETIME, SOMEWHERE.

THE PHANTOM AVENGER

5

So when Dawlish and Dexter drove the great timber wagon into town towards midnight, followed by their men, the news which greeted them was hardly encouraging. The moment he had the facts the weary Dawlish went to look at the still hanging body for himself. In grim silence he read the note affixed to it and then turned to look at the hard-faced men around him.

'No doubt of one thing, boys, we're up against it here,' he said bitterly. 'I gather you got no nearer last night trying to track the Phantom down?'

'Sheer waste of time,' Grant answered. 'Just the same as it'll be in this case, I reckon, if we attempt to do anything.'

'We're not going to attempt to,' Dawlish decided. 'He's got the drop on us every time, but what we will do, instead of chasing him, is take safety measures inside the town itself. To safeguard ourselves. Okay, cut this body down and we'll have a funeral service in the morning. Right now I'm turning in: I'm too tired to even see straight.'

And Dawlish meant what he said. The hours on the trail and the accompanying nerve strain had about brought him, temporarily anyway, to the end of his resources. He gave orders for several of the men to keep an all-night watch on the timber load — men who had not made the gruelling journey from the mountain region — and then he retired to the hotel room and remained there until break-fast time next day.

The first person he met when he got to his sheriff's office was Grant. As usual he was looking vaguely discom-fited.

'Well?' Dawlish asked him curtly, as he came in. 'Anything happen last night?'

'I guess not. Things were peaceful enough, but that doesn't change the fact that we can walk into trouble any minute or get a bullet in our backs.'

'I know that, you darned fool. That's why we've got to take precautions.'

'Sounds easy the way you put it. I reckon the Phantom will find a way to us no matter what . . . ' Grant moodily chewed at his cheroot for a moment, then: 'Who the devil is this Phantom, anyhow? Got any ideas?'

'None: I'm completely sunk.' Dawlish's brows knitted for a moment. 'It can't be Nick, or Halligan. They're both dead — and in any case neither of them would have reason for turning against us like this. They're on our side, or at any rate they were before going over the precipice.'

'No doubt about either of them being dead, I suppose?'

'Of course there's no doubt. I saw their bodies for myself, a thousand feet down on the rocks.'

'And you examined them and made sure they were dead?'

'No — too much time would have

been taken up.' Dawlish gave an irritated motion. 'What the devil are you talking about, man? They're dead — quite dead. Remember that this Phantom strung up Hennesy whilst we were still riding across the desert. Neither Halligan nor Nick could have done that without riding ahead of us and — Oh, what in blazes am I talking about? Where'd you get the crazy idea of those two being mixed up in this?'

'Dunno. Just because I can't think of anybody else, I s'pose. Who else is there?'

'I just told you — I don't know.' Dawlish was too edgy to argue further. 'We'd better see the Hennesy funeral through and then get the boys to work unloading the timber.'

Grant nodded and gloomily followed Dawlish out of the office. Throughout the funeral service and during the burial of Hennesy at the small local cemetery they were constantly on the alert for anything alarming happening — even for the crack of a long-range rifle, but nothing disturbed the peace. Evidently the Phantom was not such a fool as to risk anything when there were a number of townsfolk about. This reflection cheered Dawlish somewhat and once the burial was over he wasted no time in detailing the town's best sharpshooters to the job of keeping a constant watch on the town in general, and upon himself, Grant, and Dexter in particular. Once this was done the unloading of the timber wagon began.

Such was the start of Dawlish's uneasy campaign to establish Carterville as the centre of an oil empire. There was certainly no doubt that he had plenty of courage, harassed as he was night and day by the thought that at any moment he might be struck down. In between the complexities of directing the erection of the oil derricks he did what he could to trace the possible identity of the Phantom. It could have been one of the men of the town, one bolder than the rest, disliking

Dawlish's schemes, but in every case the trail was blind and finally Dawlish had to give it up.

He took good care that neither he, Grant, or Dexter took any long journeys alone. They stayed put in Carterville. The driving of the timber wagon, back and forth, was undertaken by tough horsemen who would surely not be worth the attention of the Phantom. Such seemed to be the case for succeeding loads came through safely enough and the oil derricks began to rise steadily in the surrounding landscape. Beholding this, Dawlish breathed a little more freely and even began to hope that his precautionary measures had decided the Phantom against further reprisals.

Then, just as Dawlish — and in a less measure Grant — had acquired this complacent state of mind a further blow fell. The news of it came on the morning when Dawlish had planned to make the first experimental borings. Everything was set. The derricks were ready, the drilling equipment was installed, then Ralph Lincoln, the man whom Dawlish had put in charge of the engineering side because of his considerable skill in this direction, arrived with his bad news.

'We can't make a start, Mr Dawlish!' Lincoln's craggy, sweating face was a mixture of frustration and anger. 'The drills have been chewed.'

Dawlish, who with Grant had been standing on the steps of the mobile headquarters hut, surveyed the derrick-straddled region in vague wonder.

'Chewed?' He snatched his cheroot from his mouth. 'What the blue hell are you talking about, man?'

Lincoln motioned back with a brawny arm to where the various workers were congregated around No. 1 derrick. At a distance from them, kept away by a wire fence, were men and women of the town anxious to see the result of the first drilling which had been so persistently announced.

'Come and take a look,' Lincoln urged.

'I never saw boring equipment in such a state.'

Muttering to himself Dawlish followed the big engineer across the dusty space and presently found himself looking at the great drill which, had things been in order, would have now begun to bore down into the earth to release the first pent-up fountain of oil. But the drill, massive though it was, was broken off like a snapped needle about halfway up its length. Of the missing end, the essential part, there was no sign.

'What about the spare drills?' Dawlish snapped.

'Smashed too, boss. We had three. Every one of them has been broken in two, and there's no sign of the lower halves anyway. Not that that would do any good. You can't repair 'em.'

Dawlish clenched his fists and gave a glance towards Grant. Grant did not say anything but his look conveyed plenty.

'It's beyond me how this could ever

have happened!' Dawlish declared finally, after another examination of the drill. 'It has been snapped off by sheer force, yet we've had a guard over these derricks and equipment night and day. Unless somebody's been asleep on the job.'

'More unlikely things than that, I reckon,' Lincoln sighed.

'And what do you mean by that?' Grant barked at him.

'Well, Mr Grant, I reckon a lot of the boys are tired. They've been workin' like hell these last few weeks, to all hours. I wouldn't blame a few of 'em for droppin' off even on guard duty.'

'You mean it is quite conceivable that somebody could have got into this area without being challenged?' Dawlish demanded.

'Yeah, that's what I mean. But how the drills have bin broken up without any sound being heard I just can't figger.'

Dawlish gave a sour smile. 'Well, I can. All these drills are as brittle as carrots: that's because of their high temper. You only need to lay them under a big rock and drop the rock on 'em and they'd snap in a second. That's no problem. Our saboteur obviously unscrewed this drill, and took the others away. He smashed 'em up, then put everything back as it was — all because the boneheads left on guard didn't do their job properly.'

'Unless one of the guards is the Phantom,' Grant pointed out, and at that Dawlish's expression changed somewhat.

'Yes, that's a possibility,' he admitted. 'Lincoln, round up every man who's been on guard duty. I'm going to put some mighty searching questions.'

Lincoln nodded and turned away. He had hardly done so before one of the workers came hurrying up, a piece of white card in his hand.

'I just found this, Mr Dawlish, amongst the broken drills. We none of us noticed it until the drills were lifted out.'

Dawlish took the card and read, Grant peering over his shoulder:

142

I'LL BREAK YOU, DAWLISH, AS YOU'VE BROKEN OTHERS. THIS IS JUST A SAMPLE FROM
THE PHANTOM AVENGER

Dawlish tightened his lips slowly and then looked at Grant.

'We can't go on fighting this kind of thing, Dawlish,' Grant said. 'We've got to get out — whilst we're still living.'

'And leave behind us a fortune in oil? Just forget all about these derricks and the labour force? Throw the lot overboard? No, Grant, we're not doing that — or at least I'm not. If you want to quit that's your own affair. I do admit that we're dealing with somebody who's damned smart, but one of these days he'll overstep himself . . . ' Dawlish glanced up when he saw Lincoln returning at the head of a body of men. 'Now maybe we will get a bit nearer the truth. The Phantom could be one of these men at that.'

But if such was the case the clues were extremely rare. Dawlish assigned himself the task of merciless cross-questioning for nearly an hour, but by the time he had finished he was no nearer than when he had started. Finally he relaxed and lighted a cheroot.

'All right, so be it,' he said bitterly. 'But I warn every one of you, if anything like this happens again I'll strike the whole crowd of you off the workers' list and be damned to the consequences.'

The men eyed him for a moment and then broke up into sullen-faced groups, muttering amongst themselves.

'Better take it easy, boss,' Lincoln warned. 'Their tempers are pretty edgy after the hours they've been working. If they get on the wrong side of you they can cause plenty of trouble — even stop the oil project altogether.'

'I have the idea that that has already been done for me,' Dawlish growled, round his cheroot. 'Just the same, I see

144

your point. Won't do to goad them too far. Right now we've got to get these drills replaced and the only way to do that is to get a new lot from Sarcot's Bend.'

'Okay,' Lincoln replied. 'I'll be on my way as soon as I can — '

'No.' Dawlish shook his head. 'Mr Grant will go, and I will stay behind and take charge.'

Grant gave a start. 'I will? What the hell's the idea? I thought we'd sworn off leaving town? Leastways, until the Phantom's been caught. You don't suppose I'm going to take a lone ride to Sarcot's Bend, do you? It'll be plain asking for it. Remember, I'm on the danger list the same as you.'

'You won't come to any harm on a trip like that,' Dawlish answered patiently. 'The desert's a big place and it just isn't possible for anybody to creep up on you. You'll have as much chance as the Phantom, if he attempted anything. Your trickiest part will be getting through the mountains, but if you keep your eyes open you should manage okay. The Phantom can only get at you there by riding ahead of you, and he sure can't do that without your seeing him. You've nothing to fear, and I've got to have a man I can trust to get those drills.'

The extra bit about a 'man he could trust' did not have much effect on Grant. The fear of a hidden bullet by far outweighed anything that flattery could do. Then, just as he was about to protest further an idea occurred to him. For long enough he had been trying to think of a way out of the iron circle into which he had been drawn. Here perhaps was a chance to ride out of it all — forget the oil, Dawlish, and everything else. To Grant's not particularly ambitious mind a little peace and quiet was far to be preferred to the constant threat of death or a fortune.

'I'm not taking any arguments, Grant,' Dawlish said flatly, as he saw his partner lost in thought. 'I know what wants doing and you're the man to do it. Sooner the better.'

'Okay, I'll go,' Grant said quietly, 'but I'm not saying that I'm looking forward to it. Can't somebody come with me? Two of us would make things easier in case of trouble.'

'I want every man and horse I can get,' Dawlish answered. 'This is one thing you've got to do alone. Come into the hut and I'll give you a repeat order form.'

Grant tightened his lips and followed Dawlish slowly. It had not occurred to him yet that Dawlish had his own reasons for wanting to be rid of him. If anything happened to Grant, Dawlish would be in sole charge of the oil project, a prospect which appealed to Dawlish more than somewhat. The grumbling, frightened Grant was commencing to get on his nerves, anyway.

'There,' Dawlish said finally, handing over a duplicate order form. 'That's all you need — and here's a cheque for the stuff. One way or another we're going to be bankrupt in a while if we keep on having to do everything twice over.'

Grant muttered something inaudible, then went on his way to make his preparations. Half-an-hour later he departed and Dawlish returned to his task of control of the labour force, concentrated for the time being in the supervision of the building of the big sectional tanks, in which he hoped the precious oil would eventually be stored. In spite of the number of factors against him Dawlish still went on stubbornly, assured within himself that he would eventually break down all opposition and emerge triumphant . . .

During this activity his main assistant was Dexter, and by and large he was not much better than Grant as far as temperament went. Knowing his name was on the Phantom's list he worked constantly with one eye metaphorically glancing behind him, but — for the moment at least — there was no sign of trouble. Probably the Phantom considered that his activities with the drills had caused trouble enough for the time being.

And out in the desert Grant rode steadily under the blazing sun, but the general direction he took was definitely not towards Sarcot's Bend, or the mountains which preceded that township. Instead, after he had covered perhaps five miles from Carterville, he left the trail proper and bore towards the north. From what he could remember of the maps he had seen the nearest big cities lay to the north — and this was what concerned him. He wanted to forsake for ever the death-trap which was Carterville and instead make an entirely new life away from the difficulties and dangers engendered entirely by Dawlish's over-riding ambition.

Grant even smiled to himself as he rode steadily onwards under the hot sun. He had got out of everything so easily — ridden out on a supposed errand — and he would never return. That this was just what Dawlish was hoping for was still something which did not occur to him.

So Grant rode onwards. He stopped at each waterhole on the northward route, and during these intervals he took the opportunity of surveying the desert carefully on all sides. But there was no sign of a living soul. Just the eternal quivering heat and the cobalt sky, a single wisp of high cirrus cloud being the only defilement on the perfect vault.

On again, until at last nightfall came. Grant had already made up his mind that he would have to sleep in the desert for there were some hundreds of miles of it yet to cross before he came anywhere near the 'civilization' he was bent on reaching. So at sundown he stopped, watered and fed his weary horse, and then made his own preparations for a meal and a rest.

He had got to the point of rolling himself a cigarette and was feeling comfortably relaxed after his meal when he fancied he caught faint sounds drifting out of the quiet of the desert. For a moment or two, as he mechanically put the finishing touches to his cigarette, he placed the noises as belonging inevitably to the desert itself — but when they changed to a certain rhythm he knew he was mistaken. Those noises were hoofbeats and he was feeling them through earth reverberations more than hearing them.

Immediately he came to the alert, his hand dropping to his gun. He threw away the unlighted cigarette and peered intently into the night. At the moment everything was masked in uniform grey — the inevitable mist of the early night, diffusing the gleam of the stars. It made directional noises difficult to pinpoint, with the result that Grant began peering in various directions, noting at the same time the increasing nearness of the hoofbeats. For a moment he considered jumping quickly on to his nearby hobbled and sleeping horse: then he changed his mind. For one thing the animal was too weary to go far, and for another the sound of its hoofs would be a direct give away. So

Grant waited, with increasing tension, his gun ready for any eventuality.

It was particularly unnerving to him to discover that, after reaching a crescendo of nearness, the hoofbeats suddenly ceased. There was not a sound disturbing the night. Yet his own horse shifted uneasily nearby, instinctively sensing something.

Grant stared fixedly into the drifting mist. He could feel his forehead become clammy with the intensity of events. Somebody was near him, somebody who had dismounted from his horse and was now probably creeping nearer —

'Drop that gun, Grant!' commanded a harsh voice.

Grant jumped in terror, swung round, then fired at the direction of the voice. A gun blazed back at him and though no bullet struck him he dropped his weapon in sheer fright. Not a second later a tall white shape came out of the mist, a figure illuminated by the starshine. It was shapeless and completely masked.

'Nice to see you scared, Grant,' the Phantom said, in his unidentifiable voice. 'You've got some idea now how many ranchers and their families felt when you and that skunk Dawlish launched your terror campaign.'

'I didn't launch anything!' Grant shouted hoarsely, feeling vainly for his gun in the sand. 'It was all Dawlish's doing. I'd nothing to do with it. In fact I was against it from the start!'

'A man who was against Dawlish wouldn't so calmly assume the office of Mayor of Carterville, Grant. That doesn't convince me for a moment. Oh no, you're one of the choice ones who've turned Carterville into the headquarters of a gang of no-account killers. But presently there won't be any killers left. I finished Hennesy, and I'll finish you. I saw you leave town and I followed at a considerable distance — a distance so great you were nothing more to me than a speck of dust in the emptiness. But that dust trail was a beacon, constantly indicating your whereabouts.

And now I've caught up!'

Grant sweated in the starlight. He did not even dare to move. He could see reflections from the Phantom's gun.

'You don't know who I am, do you?' the Phantom asked presently.

'No. No, of course I don't! You could be Halligan, or Nick, or — '

'I'm neither of them. They're finished, as they deserve. But one thing I can tell you. Though I said I brought about the end of those two and smashed the timber load, that wasn't true. They did it themselves. They started fighting and the wagon went over the cliff. I'd followed them and I saw everything that happened. No, Grant, I'm neither Nick nor Halligan: I'm somebody with far more reason than either of them to want to see you and the rest of your dirty gang wiped out.'

'Then — then who the hell are you?' Grant nearly screamed.

'That's my business.' The voice was ice cold again. 'And here is where I pay my account.'

Grant stood no chance. The Phantom's gun fired twice and Grant sank silently down to the sand. Nearby, his horse shied violently at the shots and then stood in the starlight with his ears flicking. Behind his mask the Phantom smiled bitterly to himself, releathered his gun, then dragged Grant's dead body upwards. Without any attempt at care or ceremony he slung the corpse over the nearby horse and roped it securely — then the Phantom departed to get his own mount.

Ten minutes later he was riding across the desert, trailing behind him Grant's weary horse and its dead burden . . .

★   ★   ★

Throughout the following day Dawlish was in the bitterest of moods. He had expected Grant returning long before this, and until he did come no further progress could be made with the oil project.

'Dammit,' he swore at Dexter, 'it shouldn't take him all this time to get to Sarcot and back. Not as though he has a whole wagon to control. Nothing but himself and his horse.'

'Uh-huh,' Dexter acknowledged, gazing through the hut window on to the men idling around.

'That the best comment you can make?' Dawlish demanded, and at that Dexter gave a shrug and turned to him.

'Matter of fact, Dawlish, I get the feeling all the time that you're putting on an act. I don't believe you're half so bothered about Grant not returning as you make out.'

'Don't talk like a fool! We've got to have the drills, haven't we?'

'Oh, sure, we've got to have the drills — but if they don't arrive I guess somebody else can go and get 'em. I don't think you want Grant to come back, and the reason's plain enough. Without him you don't have to share the profits of this potential oil empire you've got. You've got nobody to worry

156

about except me.'

Dawlish started, staring fixedly at Dexter's round, determined face.

'Except you! You've never been a partner in this project and you never will be.'

'No?' Dexter raised an eyebrow. 'I'm not the same as the others, Dawlish, and you know it. I rank on the same plane as Nick, Halligan, and Grant, and I'm standing for my rights. You've been quick enough to rope me in as your assistant while Grant isn't here, and I demand that that assistance be recognized! You're not dealing with some no-account cowpoke, remember. I've a certain amount of education and a good deal of business sense. I'm telling you here and now — you've got yourself a partner.'

'And when Grant returns how do you suppose he'll take it?' Dawlish snapped.

'I don't give a damn how he takes it. You, Grant, and me are the sole bosses of this project and that's all there is to be said. Besides, if Grant doesn't return there'll be another mayor needed and I'm the only possible man for the job.'

Dawlish did not say anything, but inwardly he somewhat unreasonably cursed the fates which seemed to be working against him. He felt pretty sure that Grant must have fallen foul of the Phantom Avenger, but he certainly had not reckoned with the usually quiet and unobtrusive Dexter muscling in in this fashion. Besides, he did not trust Dexter. Grant had always been too scared to act very much on his own initiative — but not Dexter. There were hidden and probably dangerous depths in the man.

'Well, there it is,' Dexter said finally. 'Now I'd better go and find something for this bunch of idlers to do. They can't just stand around wasting time.'

Dawlish made some kind of inaudible response and lighted a cheroot. And, for the remainder of the day, he was constantly on edge. On the one hand he awaited Grant's possible return; on the other he had to be on the alert for a possible attack from the Avenger. And around him the men did odd jobs and waited and the derricks towered to the cobalt sky. Dexter for his part did not have very much to say. Evidently he considered that he had his position clear enough . . .

Then towards nightfall, just after sunset, things began to happen. Dawlish was in the hut at the time, scowling and thinking in the light of the oil lamp, when Dexter suddenly burst in upon him.

'Grant's here!' Dexter announced.

'Oh, he is!' Dawlish got to his feet, not sure whether to feel annoyed or relieved. 'And about time — '

'But he's dead,' Dexter added grimly. 'His horse just came staggering in, about out on its feet. From the look of things Grant's been dead some hours. Here — this was pinned on him. The same old routine, I guess.'

Dexter threw down a white card on the rough table and Dawlish read it in silence:

GRANT IS RETURNED TO YOU FOR
BURIAL. I WOULD NOT SUFFER
THE TROUBLE OF DEFILING THE
GROUND BY DOING IT MYSELF.
THE LIST IS SHORTER NOW.
              THE PHANTOM AVENGER

'You'd better come and look,' Dexter said.

Dawlish savagely tore the card in pieces and then strode out after Dexter into the area of lights cast by the kerosene lamps. A murmuring band of men was gathered around an exhausted horse, upon which was tied Grant's body. It hadn't taken Dawlish above a moment to ascertain that Grant had been dead some hours — and the two bullet wounds in head and chest were sufficient evidence as to the cause.

'From the look of things,' Dexter said, 'he never even got to Sarcot's Bend. The broken drills are still in his pack. The Phantom must have brought Grant and his horse this far, and then set the horse travelling this way.'

'That's about the size of it, Mr Dexter,' agreed engineer Lincoln, in the forefront of the assembled men. Then he looked at Dawlish. 'Well, Mr Dawlish, what do we do now? Abandon the whole thing?'

'Abandon it?' Dawlish repeated, astonished. 'What on earth are you talking about?'

'I'm talking for myself and the rest of the men, Mr Dawlish. It's pretty plain there's a jinx in this lot, and once we get that nobody's very keen on carrying on. Begins to look to me as though this Phantom Avenger has got us licked.'

'That may be your defeatist opinion, but it isn't mine,' Dawlish retorted. 'We're carrying straight on, in spite of the further delays this is going to cause. Get Grant's body unfastened and we'll bury him tomorrow morning with a proper service. During tonight I want six men, all good gunmen, to go to Sarcot and do the job which Grant failed to do. We've got to have fresh drills at the earliest moment.'

'You do well to call for volunteers,' Lincoln commented dryly. 'In view of what's happened a journey like that seems to me to be an invitation to certain death.'

Dawlish shook his head. 'Not for six good gunmen. I reckon even the Phantom wouldn't tackle that proposition. And in any case he would have no incentive to do so. He's made it perfectly clear that he's wiping out the high-ups — of which only two remain. Dexter here, and myself. But I'm not afraid of him, or his imaginary grievance.'

'The way things are going,' Lincoln said slowly, 'it sorta makes one wonder if the Phantom's grievance is so imaginary. He seems to have gotten the idea that you high level gentlemen have been up to something mighty questionable.'

'He believes,' Dawlish answered, scenting danger, 'that men in control of things were also responsible for the destruction of the various ranches around here, and the deaths of the families concerned — but that is absolute rubbish. We had nothing to do with that. Indeed, as many townsfolk will tell you, Grant and I were the ones who did our best to save the town from catching fire, for which we were elected to the offices of mayor and sheriff.'

'I see,' Lincoln said, but he sounded faraway about it.

'And that brings up another matter,' Dexter put in. 'What do we do about a new mayor? I'm not trying to push anything, but now Grant has been murdered I seem to be the logical successor.'

'We'll put it to the townsfolk tomorrow when we have the funeral,' Dawlish decided. 'And now, the rest of you, I'm still waiting for volunteers.'

None of the men moved, but they glanced at each other.

'I'll put it another way,' Dawlish continued deliberately. 'All of you expect to be paid your wages, since the fact that you have no immediate work to do is not your own fault. You'll get

163

those wages only if we have the drills. I'm not a magician. I can't produce oil and be paid for it without the equipment with which to do it. In your own interests you'd better do something.'

'All right, we will,' Lincoln decided abruptly. 'I'll volunteer to lead a party to Sarcot and back. Who's with me? I only need five men.'

After a few minutes he got them. He nodded and turned back to Dawlish.

'We'll do it, Mr Dawlish, and be back as quick as can be. And I'm sorry for what I said just now.'

'Said?'

'Yeah — when I sort of questioned whether the Phantom might not have a real grievance. Obviously he's loco, and if we see him anywheres on the way we'll blast hell out of him — ' He swung. 'All right, you volunteers. Start makin' your preparations.'

6

For the men of the untapped oil region, and also for Dawlish and Dexter, there was nothing further could be done that night so, once having transported the body of Grant into town in a crude, hastily made coffin, they retired to the Journey's End, mainly at Dexter's suggestion.

It was not long before Dawlish discovered why. Fully assured that he would be made mayor upon the morrow Dexter's aim was to discover what kind of an 'inheritance' he was walking into, as far as the financial side was concerned. Before he fully grasped what was happening Dawlish found himself exposing to view the profits of the Journey's End, to say nothing of the other properties he had acquired by fair means or foul.

'Yeah, good enough,' Dexter decided,

upon reflection. 'One might do a durned sight worse than be mayor of this town, Dawlish. I never figgered there was so much in it otherwise I might have contested Grant's nomination for mayor.'

Dawlish closed up the books and made no comment. Inwardly he had already had more than enough of Dexter: he could see in him the nucleus of a great deal of friction in the future.

'Bet you're none too keen on a partner, eh, Dawlish?' Dexter grinned, as they both turned to the office door. 'One man alone running most of this town — as you're in a position now to do — could make the hell of a lot without benefit of oil thrown in. For some things I'm more'n glad I'm the only one left of the other mob.'

Dawlish did not take the matter up. Instead he said:

'I've some special work to do, Dexter, and I'm doing it at my hotel room where I can't be disturbed. Since you're as good as my partner now keep your eye on things here tonight. Right?'

'Right,' Dexter agreed affably. 'See you at Grant's funeral in the morning.'

Dawlish gave a nod and went on his way, leaving Dexter to handle things as he saw fit. Which he did, taking care to serve Dexter well in the process. He ordered what drink he required and made no effort to pay for it; and at the same time he kept an eye on how much money went into the till. Yes, he was going to like this partnership more than somewhat, and to hell with the threat of the Phantom Avenger. So he continued to preen himself and remained in the saloon until closing time. By then he was more than slightly fuddled and it took him all his time to find the way across the main street to the room he had in the same hotel as Dawlish.

He was humming to himself as he unlocked the bedroom door and stumbled into the gloom beyond — then something, he was not sure what, sobered him very slightly. He became instinctively aware of some hidden danger.

'Can't be,' he muttered thickly to himself. 'Ain't no danger here. Reckon this is the safest place in town . . . '

Just the same he stopped singing and instead lighted the oil lamp quickly. The moment the flame burned up he gave a violent start. Seated in the solitary chair by the window — over which the curtains had been drawn — was Dawlish. He looked completely at his ease but there was a menacing glint in his eyes.

'Huh! You!' Dexter exclaimed, swaying slightly. 'An' what the hell do you want in my room? Or don't y'know it's time the both of us was in bed?'

'I know quite a few things,' Dawlish replied calmly, 'and in particular I know that there are few men on earth whom I dislike as much as you, Dexter. It was different with the others — Halligan, Nick, Grant, and the rest of them. They didn't push things too much — but you're like a blasted ferret the way you spend the time rooting out details of this and that.'

'A coming mayor and partner in an oil corporation has to know all the facts,' Dexter said, with intoxicated majesty.

'That's a matter of opinion. Fact is I've decided I don't want you as a partner, and the things and people I don't want I remove. I've always been like that.'

'Have you now?' Dexter caught hold of the bed-rail and waited for the next.

'It so happens that I'm given a very unique opportunity here,' Dawlish continued, getting to his feet. 'The whole town knows that you and I are on the list of the Phantom Avenger — so if you were rubbed out the explanation would be simple, wouldn't it? Particularly with one of the Phantom's characteristic cards pinned on your chest. Not a soul in the world would suspect me of being responsible.'

'So that's it!' An ugly look came to Dexter's flushed face and his hand dropped clumsily to his gun. Before he could draw it the butt of Dawlish's own

169

gun crashed down on his skull and he flattened to the floor. For Dawlish, the remainder was cold, methodical murder. From around his waist he unwound a length of tough cord, tossed it over the broad beam crossing the ceiling, and then noosed it. And the remainder was simply a replica of the fate which had overtaken Hennesy.

When Dawlish crept out silently to his own room in the hotel he left behind him Dexter's swinging corpse and a note pinned to his chest, written in characters almost indistinguishable from the Phantom's own style. Dawlish was well satisfied. The last piece of opposition — barring the Phantom himself of course — had been eliminated from his path. So he went to bed and slept without a single qualm.

Next morning the hanging body was found, of course, and as sheriff Dawlish quickly found the case being handed over to him. With due solemnity he examined the situation, recorded all the facts, and then promised to do what he could. Not that the townsfolk expected much, having become inured by this time to the Phantom's immunity from capture.

Nonetheless, Dawlish went through all the motions of a sheriff trying to gather evidence. He asked innumerable questions and examined Dexter's room carefully — but finally he had to admit himself beaten, and as he had expected, none of the townsfolk raised any word against him.

Then, towards evening, Lincoln and his boys came riding back into town. Dawlish was in his hut at the oil project when the men arrived and he found himself anxiously counting the riders as they came in. There were six, with Lincoln — the same number which had started out. He smiled to himself, went to the doorway, and waited for Lincoln, dusty and tired, as he came hurrying up; carrying what were evidently the new drills in a tarpaulin covering.

'Well, boss, I guess we made it.' He strode past Dawlish and deposited the drills on the office desk. 'Never a sign of anybody, either going or coming. But it sure is one hell of a journey.'

'I knew you'd be safe,' Dawlish responded, coming over to him. 'Chiefly because even the Phantom can't be in two places at once — and since he's been busy here he couldn't be attacking you and your men at the same time.'

'You mean — again?' Lincoln's craggy face was startled.

'I do. This time he got Dexter, in his hotel last night. He was found strung up to a ceiling beam with the usual note pinned on his chest. This time the note said: 'There's only Dawlish left'. At which I suppose I am expected to be reduced to a nervous wreck.' Dawlish laughed shortly. 'Our murderous acquaintance greatly underestimates me. Dexter's funeral was this morning. In fact, funerals keep happening so regularly it's beginning to have a depressing effect on the townsfolk.'

'I can imagine.' Lincoln looked gloomy for a moment or two, but then he brightened up again. 'Anyways, we've won the battle so far, boss, thanks to you refusing to be shaken. I got all the new drills we need and we're all set to go. You just say the word.'

'I shan't say it until tomorrow morning. You and the boys need a long rest after what you've done, so you're off duty until tomorrow morning. See to it, though, that a full guard is kept over everything, including these drills, during tonight. And I mean men who'll stay awake!'

Lincoln nodded and picked the drills up again. 'I'll see to it, boss. There won't be any slip-ups this time.'

Nor indeed were there. Dawlish had no idea whether the Phantom knew that fresh drills had been obtained, but whatever the circumstances no attempt was made to ruin the duplicates. And the guard, as Dawlish had demanded, remained constantly on the alert. All the men had come to realize by now that unless this oil project succeeded they were in danger of losing their jobs.

Then, at nine the next morning, Dawlish got things on the move. He gave Lincoln his orders and the squads of men, glad of the end of idleness, went to work. Since most of the townsfolk knew that this was the day when they would know whether there was to be an oil yield or not, they collected around the enclosed area to watch the proceedings.

Dawlish spent more anxious moments than he had ever done so far, supervising the activity of his men. For him too the hour of crisis was very near. If there was a yield — and he felt sure there would be — everything would be plain sailing. The people would trust him until he got the other yields working, and there would also be a return of the money he had liberally spent to get the project started. He was in debt to the townsfolk to the tune of some thousands of dollars, so certainly something had got to happen quickly to straighten things out.

And at approximately eleven-thirty

something did happen. The final details were complete and engineer Lincoln 'O'd' his finger and thumb in a signal to Dawlish who was standing nearby.

'Right!' Dawlish gave a brief nod, and then stood waiting tensely.

Immediately the master drill went into operation. For some moments there was no sound except the whining of the drilling machinery; then there came a different kind of noise — a deep bass rumbling that set many of the people instinctively backing away.

The underground sound deepened; then it began to climb up the scale. There was a moment when everything seemed to hang in the balance . . . then out came the oil, a titanic gusher spraying in a black cloud to the top of the derrick and swamping the engineers and spectators who were to windward of it.

Thicker it came, and thicker still — tons of it. Brown-black rain, descending in a deluge. For a few brief seconds there were shouts of alarm, then these changed to cries of delight as men and women seized hold of each other in hysterical joy and began a crazy capering. Oil! Oil! Tens of thousands of dollars were about to roll into this backwoods little township . . . Dawlish, speckled with oil spots, grinned as he heard his name being called in praise. He was the man of the hour, the one who had foresight and courage enough to unlock the wealth that lay below this arid, sun-fried little spot.

'All right, cap it down!' he yelled, signalling to Lincoln. 'We've got what we want for the moment.'

Lincoln nodded and signalled to his men. Within a few minutes the massive cap had been swung into place over the bore and the fountain ceased. Men and women came floundering through the sticky, slippery lake which lay to windward of the derrick and Dawlish found himself seized by exultant hands.

'Congratulations, boss!' Lincoln grinned. 'You did it — and I guess this is only the first of several.'

'You can say that again,' Dawlish smiled.

'Nice work, boss!'

'Three cheers for Sheriff Dawlish!'

Dawlish stood in silence for a moment or two, soaking in the eulogy; then when the cheering had died down he turned again to Lincoln.

'Start getting the boys busy on the rest of the plan,' he ordered. 'We want our mobile railway put in action as fast as possible. Whilst that's being done start loading up the oil storage tanks. You know the lay-out: we've been through it time and again ready for this moment. I've got a special job to do: inform the Texas Company that we're ready to start delivery. The moment I've cleaned myself up I'll be on my way.'

'Is that a safe thing to do?' Lincoln asked seriously. 'In spite of this success don't forget the Phantom.'

'To hell with the Phantom!' Dawlish retorted. 'I'll take my chance on that. Get busy, Lincoln. I'll be back as soon as I can . . .'

* * *

And, for the time being at least, the luck seemed to be on Dawlish's side. Although he fully expcted an attack when he took the lone trail of the desert, the expectancy did not materialise. He arrived in Sarcot's Bend in the late evening, stayed the night, and then went on to the oil company next morning. By ten-thirty he was in the office of Morgan Ayres, the big man who not only controlled that particular company but several others as well. Dawlish was not sure whether he felt pleased by this fact or not: so far he had not had any direct dealings with the boss of bosses. Still, the buying arrangement had been made, so he plunged straight away into business.

'My Carterville oil project has started yielding,' he explained, when the cigars were under way. 'There's nothing now standing in the way of us transporting the oil to you at the agreed figure. As fast as we produce it, you can have it.'

178

'I see.' Ayres meditated, a bulldog of a man who certainly would never say yes if he meant no. 'I am of course glad for your sake that your enterprise has succeeded, but as far as we are concerned there have been serious internal reverses. Financial and distribution troubles.' Ayres spread his hands and grinned unconvincingly round his cigar. 'You know how it is.'

Dawlish's expression changed. 'I'm afraid I don't. You have a contract with me to buy all the oil I can produce to add to your own reserves.'

Ayres' grin did not disappear. If anything it widened.

'I'm sorry to have to tell you, Mr Dawlish, that that contract isn't really valid. Mind you, we would have conformed to it had our own affairs been in order, but as it is — '

'What the hell are you talking about?' Dawlish snapped. 'Not valid? Of course it's valid!'

Ayres lifted it from the stack of papers at his elbow and spread it out on the blotter. With a fat finger he indicated the signatories.

'No deed concerning this multi-corporation is valid unless it has my signature. This has not. In some cases the signatures of the Texas Company's two partners are enough — as they probably believed it would be on this occasion, but in a point of law my own signature seals the matter. In this instance I did not sign. You would not be aware of the omission at the time and assumed everything was in order.'

Dawlish jumped to his feet. 'What kind of a crooked deal is this? Without your organisation as my buyer how the devil do I get rid of my oil at a profit?'

'That, I am afraid, is a matter for your business ingenuity. And — ' Ayres' bulldog face became grim ' — this is not a crooked deal. I have told you why we can't buy your oil yield. You could have forced this issue if this contract had had my signature. As it is I can step out — and I'm going to. Sorry.'

Dawlish, for once, could not think of

anything to say. He certainly did not know that, because Halligan had been wiped out in his endeavours to wreck Dawlish's plans, the Texas Company no longer had any interest in the proceedings. Either they wanted to own the Carterville yield, or else forget about it entirely. The contract had been a fake in the first place, but there was no possible way by which Dawlish could have known that. He was now in the midst of that bitter discovery.

'Very well,' Dawlish said at last, stubbing out his cigar in the ash-tray. 'Maybe it's as well the way it is. I'd sooner you'd reveal the swindle now and stop my dealing with you, than reveal it later.'

Ayres did not say anything — and finally neither did Dawlish. Controlling his fury as best he could he left the office and slammed the door behind him . . . By the time he arrived back in Sarcot's Bend, where he intended to lunch before starting the return journey, he was a much troubled man. He had tapped wealth, yes — but it could never become wealth unless somebody was willing to pay for the oil.

Other oil companies? Well — yes. Dawlish thought things out as he ate his lunch. The trouble was that most, if not all, the oil concerns in this particular region were under the Texas banner, and that inevitably meant Ayres at the head. The independent companies were so far away that transport loomed as the biggest obstacle. Altogether, Dawlish was up against it, yet not for a moment did it ever occur to him that this major setback might be partial retribution for his own wrongdoing. He still had not solved the problem when he began the long ride home — all of which proved uneventful as far as attack was concerned — and his thoughts were still wrestling with the problem when he told engineer Lincoln of the devastating results of his visit.

'Well, I reckon that puts us in the devil of a mess, Mr Dawlish,' the engineer said, scratching his head. 'No use to keep bringing up oil when we've no means of disposing of it. And I reckon we can't distribute the stuff ourselves. The cost of overheads and transport would liquidate us.'

'There's one other possible solution,' Dawlish said. 'I've been thinking about it all the way home. It's an enormous proposition — but so are most things which are worthwhile. It all depends if the folks will stand beside me.'

'I reckon they will, after this gusher we've hit. What's this new angle you've got?'

'The nearest oil distribution centre to here is Willard's Acres. That's a distance of about a hundred and fifty miles over nothing else but desert. Several of the Texas combines have their distribution centres there, chiefly because the railroad passes through Willard's Acres. The Texas people load their oil on to rail tankers, after which it is transported to the refineries in the nearest cities. After that comes further distribution and sale to the transport and automobile, combines, and so forth . . . '

'Yeah,' Lincoln acknowledged, pondering. 'That's right enough. So what?'

'So this: we haven't got the necessary tankers for transporting oil across the desert. Had we dealt with Texas they would have sent their own tankers. Nor are we likely to be able to get tankers. Ayres will see to that. He'll crack down on a possible rival source of oil wherever he can. But he wouldn't be able to do anything about a pipeline. At least he would, but we'd take darned good care he didn't.'

'A pipeline? Over a hundred and fifty miles of desert?'

'Yes.' Dawlish gave a stubborn nod. 'I said it was an enormous proposition.'

'It's more than enormous,' Lincoln protested. 'I'd say it's impossible.'

'Once you admit the word 'impossible' into your vocabulary, Lincoln, you're lost! And in any case you're wrong. I admit it's a mighty big idea, but it's not impossible if we use pumping stations. Here — let's work out an estimate and see what we get. The supplies can be got from Sarcot's Bend. There are three or four big metal foundries there, I noticed.'

Looking vaguely dubious the engineer sat down and began to figure on a scratch-pad. For him it was a matter of engineering possibilities, an exact science of lengths and stresses. For Dawlish it was a problem in economics, a jigsaw of balancing his existing resources against those which he hoped would accrue later. And for nearly an hour both men worked steadily, discarding this and replacing that, working out a kind of cooperative blueprint between them to conquer a hundred and fifty miles of desert.

'From the engineering angle it can be done,' Lincoln said finally. 'But I've taken some mighty long chances in arriving at that conclusion. I've assumed a constantly working labour force and have made the minimum allowance for accidents and replacement of men. Add to that the transport problems and cost of pumping stations and materials, and I expect you'll find we're ways beyond possibility.'

'No — I don't think so.' Dawlish studied his own mathematics and then the specification list which Lincoln had worked out. 'We shall have to swing a lot of this on credit, and I think we can do it because we've got security in the oil we can produce. Any businessman knows his money's safe if there's oil in the picture. We're a tremendous investment, and my next job is to find somebody who'll back the pipeline.'

'For instance?' Lincoln enquired.

'There's a man I know in New Orleans — Haslam by name — who I think would help out. He knows I'm an oil man and he trusts my judgment. Since he's got more money than he knows what to do with he ought to be worth a visit. I'd better ride out tomorrow and see him.'

'Okay. And again take a gamble with the Phantom?'

Dawlish laughed contemptuously. 'Certainly! He didn't dare to show his face during these last trips I've been making, did he?'

'No, but — Well, just take care, boss. Without you to direct things we're liable to get tangled up.'

'Economically maybe, but not on the engineering side. You're a good oil engineer, Lincoln, and know all the tricks of the situation.'

'And on a trip that far you'll be gone some time. What am I to tell the boys and townsfolk?'

'Simply tell them the truth — that Texas won't live up to their obligations, so we're going to try and build a pipeline. You can explain that I'm trying to arrange the financial end.'

'Good enough.' Lincoln got to his feet. 'I'll do that. And I'll see that nobody gets near anything, night or day. Meantime we can start getting things ready to tap oil on the other bores we've made.'

★   ★   ★

Dawlish was nothing if not energetic. He was off again at sunup, duly provisioned and armed against attack, taking with him the estimate and details of the proposed pipeline — then there began for him that long, lonely journey eastwards towards the state of Louisiana. He knew when he started the immensity of the trip before him, but that fact did nothing to alleviate the boring monotony, the grilling heat, and the uneasy slumbers under the stars when he half expected an attack coming out of the mist. In all he had to cover half of Texas and most of Louisiana in order to reach the eastern seaboard on the Gulf of Mexico. It was in consequence a grimy, bearded, and desperately tired man and horse which finally arrived in New Orleans.

Rest — night and day — for both man and animal, then Dawlish recovered, made himself as neat as possible, and went forth from his hotel to seek Jonathan Haslam. He ran an office in the town centre where he operated under the glamorous title of 'Financial Consultant'. At least it found him something to do: a man with his resources had no need to work at all.

'Well, if it isn't Dawlish!' was Haslam's greeting, as Dawlish entered the office. 'Haven't seen you for — Oh, how long?' Haslam got up, came round the desk and shook hands vigorously. 'Must be five years. You and that fellow Grant went off oil prospecting, or something.'

'Right,' Dawlish assented. 'And for five years we've been chasing the damned stuff. Grant even lost his life in the effort but I'm still going. What's more important still, I've found oil.'

'You have?' Haslam motioned to a chair, then pushed cigars across. 'Well, it sounds as though you didn't spend your time in vain anyways . . . What's the situation? Passing through and thought you'd look me up, or is there more to it than that?'

'A great deal more, Jon. I've got oil but can't transport it due to a let-down by a potential buyer. I stand to make tens of thousands of dollars, but to do it I want backing.'

'Oh . . . ' Something of Haslam's earlier geniality had gone now. 'So you come to me?'

'Why not? You're a friend — and you're certainly not short of money. Here's my proposition . . . ' Dawlish spread out sketches, estimates, and specifications on the desk. 'A pipeline from my oil centre to the nearest distribution centre. A hundred and fifty miles at an estimated cost of two hundred thousand dollars. Once we get that pipeline through neither Texas Oil or anybody else can move as fast as us on delivery. To make doubly sure we'll undercut them in price. Nothing to stop it because I'm running an independent company.'

'Mmmm. Two hundred thousand, eh? And what's your collateral?'

'Oil! You couldn't want better collateral than that.'

'Yes, I admit it's good security — but I'd have to see the layout for myself before advancing a cent. Not that I don't trust an old friend, but I'm a businessman same as you.'

'Sure, sure,' Dawlish agreed, showing no visible annoyance that his word of itself was not enough. 'Look the thing over any time you like. Sooner the better.'

Haslam turned to a date pad and consulted it, then at length he nodded.

'Seems to me there's no time like the present. I've no important dates for two days. You ready to ride straight back or have you any other business around here?'

'None at all. I came exclusively to find you.'

Haslam grinned. 'Which seems to

suggest you must need me mighty badly. Okay, let's see what we can do about it.'

He wasted no more time. He gave a few instructions to the girl who acted as his secretary in the outer office, then he and Dawlish got on their way once they had obtained horses from the local livery stable.

In some ways Dawlish was glad of the length of the trip because it gave him a chance to build up his case at leisure. On the other hand he was apprehensive lest there might be an attack from the Phantom. This, however, did not happen throughout the long day's riding which brought them to the small township of Liberty on the eastern borders of Texas. Here they spent the night, riding on again on fresh horses shortly after sunup.

So, by evening, they arrived at Carterville, but no business was done. For one thing they were too exhausted: for another, Haslam insisted on viewing the whole set-up by daylight. So beyond exchanging a short conversation with Lincoln — from which he learned that nothing abnormal had happened — Dawlish had to let things lie for the moment.

But he was on the job early next day, Lincoln at his side to bolster things up. Not that Haslam appeared to be listening to the sales-talk being pressed upon him. He wandered around the oil site area, inspecting, making notes, asking questions, and then spending long intervals meditating. It was a short demonstration of No. 1 gusher with the cap removed which finally seemed to satisfy him.

'All right, I'll take a gamble,' he said frankly. 'I've been taking them all my life so I may as well take another.'

Dawlish rubbed his hands. 'Good! I thought you'd be satisfied when you saw what I've got. Come over to the office and we'll talk business.'

Lincoln caught the jerk of the head which was given to him and went on his way whilst Dawlish strode over to the headquarters hut. When Haslam had followed him in he motioned to the spare chair and closed the door.

'No doubt that you've got something,' Haslam mused, snipping the end from a cigar. 'There's also no doubt that with a pipeline you could become a dangerous rival to Texas in a very short time. That is when you get all your wells working. I assume that your engineer, Lincoln, will be well able to take care of all the technical details.'

'One of the best oil engineers I know. No trouble in that direction. As I told you my only handicap is financing the pipe. I've drained enough out of the Carterville pool and I daren't take any more.'

'Uh-huh; I see your difficulty. All right, you asked for two hundred thousand dollars. I'll back you for that — or for less or more, according to which way the estimate swings. I shall not give you a cheque for the amount. Instead, order all that is necessary and have the bills sent to me.'

'I — see.' There was marked hesitation in Dawlish's voice, and Haslam's eyebrows rose a little.

'What's the matter? Doesn't that satisfy you?'

'Oh sure it does. Somehow I'd expected that I'd handle everything myself and that you would loan the money, charging an interest rate.'

'I'm not going to charge a cent of interest. Instead I'm going to lay it down as a condition that I become your partner in this enterprise.'

Dawlish, who was in the act of lighting his cigar, dropped the match abruptly. He gave a hard stare.

'Partner! But I don't want a partner!'

'But you want the money, don't you? Beggars can't be choosers, Dawlish.'

Dawlish struck another match and lighted his cigar slowly, scowling at the flame. Having rid himself of all those likely to share his potential wealth he now found himself hamstrung with another leech.

'It's entirely up to you,' Haslam

continued, his mood changing slightly. 'From what I've seen I can picture a fortune coming from this region if it's handled properly. I'm not saying you won't be able to handle it single-handed: no doubt you will. But since I'm putting up the cash to make this fortune possible I'm also going to have my stake in. Take it or leave it.'

Dawlish shrugged, notions of unexpected 'accidents' drifting around in his mind.

'You leave me no choice. Okay, partner it is.'

'There's still one other condition,' Haslam continued, getting to his feet. 'I'll have a clause inserted in our agreement to the effect that in the event of anything happening to you I automatically become the owner and controller of this enterprise.'

The thought of the Phantom crossed Dawlish's mind, to be almost immediately replaced by another speculation.

'Why limit it to anything happening to me?' he questioned. 'You're as liable to sudden death as I am.'

'True, but I'm the junior partner. You're virtually in control and normally, without a special clause, I might have legal difficulty in establishing my claim to take over where you leave off.'

'Make it a two-way clause,' Dawlish said. 'Then if you are somehow eliminated I can promptly establish my right to whatever you may have accrued in the way of profits.'

'Done!' Haslam nodded. 'That settles it then. Get ahead with your pipeline and I'll honour all the bills that arrive. In the meantime I'll get my lawyer to draw up the deed. Come over and see me in a week's time: by then I should have everything ready.'

Dawlish nodded and smiled. He had by now as good as made up his mind that an 'accident' was going to happen to Haslam very quickly.

7

Haslam, though, to Dawlish's increasing annoyance, was not quite the easy target Dawlish had hoped. For one thing he remained in New Orleans and made no attempt to discover how the pipeline was going on. The only information he received concerning it was when Dawlish went over to New Orleans to sign the deed of partnership. After which Dawlish rode home again, trying to work out how to be rid of a man who seemed determined to stay hundreds of miles away from him.

Well, perhaps it did not signify so much at the moment. The time to worry would be when Haslam started to collect his share of the profits. Right now he was doing nothing but paying out, so of course, nothing must happen to him just yet.

In the end Dawlish shelved his grim

schemes for the time being and instead concentrated, with engineer Lincoln, on the supervision of the pipeline once the first pipe deliveries started to come through. And it was at this point that there began the most gruelling task Dawlish's labour gang had yet undertaken, the task of fighting the desert, the blazing sunlight, and also keeping a night and day guard over an everlengthening pipe. True there were no attempts at sabotage or interference, but the men found it hard going. More than one would have quit had it not been for the high wages which Dawlish, thanks to Haslam, was able to pay.

And the pipe became longer and longer, each section bolted into place and resting on short, thick wooden cradles, whilst back at the oil centre itself Lincoln's best men worked on the task of getting each oil well and pumping station into action for the day when the full flood would need to be sent across one hundred and fifty miles of wilderness.

Dawlish, when he thought about the Phantom at all, had come to the conclusion that this avenger had met with some mishap, or else had called off his campaign of reprisal. It did not seem that there could be any other explanation for his continued absence — unless it was all part of a scheme to produce a sense of false security. In this respect, however, Dawlish did not intend to be caught napping, hence his night and day guard over the pipeline, and also the precaution he took to travel with fully loaded guns whenever he had a distance to cover.

The progress of his activities had reached the point now where he had to make many solo jaunts to Willard's Acres for the purpose of seeing the controllers of the distribution centre. Nor did he have any difficulty in getting matters squared up to his liking. The Director of Distribution was more than willing to do business with an organization which could supply their oil through a pipeline, and at less cost than the other combines. The difficulties of transport were swept away and the necessary concessions to carry the pipeline into Willard's Acres were readily granted.

Dawlish had every reason to feel satisfied with himself by the time his arrangements were completed. The only thing he did fear, and this but vaguely, was that the other oil companies would take some kind of revenge, perhaps even to the extent of wrecking his pipeline. But in this Dawlish was betraying his own perpetual line of thought: it did not occur to him that other firms would have scruples and, rather than destroy another firm's handiwork, would instead invoke legal means to try and save themselves.

These legal pressures were brought to bear upon Dawlish as soon as his rivals gathered what he was up to. Various law-books were dusted off and regulations governing desert and adjacent territory were brought to light after nearly a century of obscuration. Time and again Dawlish found himself legally 'restrained' from crossing this or that piece of territory, because of ancient ownership laws — but he always found a way round, literally, even though it did mean considerable extra expense for more piping and the tearing down of existing pipe-track.

But still the pipe grew, snaking away from the waiting wells near Carterville into the heart of the bleaching desert. Month after month the men toiled under the cobalt blue of the sky, most of them cursing the pipeline and everything connected with it — but sticking to the job because they knew their livelihood depended on it.

And, most of the time, Dawlish was there too. Grimy, sweating, he did not shirk any of his responsibilities, so nobody else felt they had much right to say anything . . . And so to the ninth month from the day of starting, and by this time the weather was cooler but still sunny — and the pipeline's end was only half a mile from the distribution centre. It stretched away as a black line straight across the desert and vanished over the horizon where lay Carterville. The project was all but completed. A matter of a week would see the end.

'Yes, I reckon we've done well,' Dawlish commented, as he, Lincoln, and several of the leading workmen looked back across the desert from the edge of Willard's Acres.

'No doubt of it,' Lincoln commented. 'I figgered when you first mentioned the idea, Mr Dawlish, that it was going to be too much of a job, but once again your imagination was right. Half-a-mile to go and the thing's finished . . . I've only one worry. We can guard the pumping stations, but not the whole hundred and fifty miles of pipe.'

'We won't attempt to,' Dawlish responded. 'Our competitors have given up trying to crush us by legal means, and I'm sure they won't attempt sabotage.'

'Maybe they won't, but what about the Phantom?'

'I think we can safely discount him by now. All these months have gone by and there's been no trace nor sign of him. He may even be dead, or else he realizes that the opposition is too strong for him . . . '

'I hope it is so, Mr Dawlish,' Lincoln muttered, 'because if he once got at this pipeline and smashed it we'd be thrown back months putting things straight again.'

'That's one of the risks, Lincoln, if risk it is. And as for your saying we cannot guard this pipeline, you're unduly pessimistic. We can do so by day, if not by night. Half-a-dozen men along the length can easily see to the horizon without difficulty — and any person stands out black against the sand. By night it's different, and but for the prohibitive cost we might devise some kind of searchlight system.' Dawish thought about this for a moment or two and then shook his head. 'No, forget it. We'll take our chance by night.'

And so it had to be, but apparently without any trouble being experienced. No attacks were made and the final half-mile of pipeline was completed, leading directly to the giant storage tanks which the Distributors had had erected in Willard's Acres. The hour had come at last for the final ceremony, and of course the principal men concerned were Dawlish, Haslam — lured from New Orleans specially for the occasion — and engineer Lincoln. Back at their Carterville base, connected by roughly slung land-phone, the engineers awaited the signal to release the oil.

'This, my friends, is a wonderful thing you have accomplished,' declared the Director of Distribution, as he and the others stood on the bunting-bedecked platform at the edge of the Centre. 'You have shown an incredible initiative and perseverance in bringing this pipeline across a hundred and fifty miles of wilderness — and we are doubly grateful insofar that we, as well as you, are the recipients of the oil. My sincere congratulations . . . '

Dawlish murmured a few words, feeling conspicuous. Not that he was shy but the cloud of the Phantom had once more crossed his mind. Standing here he was just a waiting target, so he hurried through the preliminaries as rapidly as possible. With this done he picked up the telephone beside him and gave the word of release.

After that the results were rapid. The oil had come sweeping through in a matter of minutes, emptying itself into the giant tanks waiting to receive it. The delivery of the first consignment was complete, and when finally both the tanks were full the supply was cut off and for Dawlish there was waiting the first cheque — and a substantial one — as reward for his endeavours.

For a moment or two, as he held the cheque in his hand, he was almost happy — but only for a moment or two. Two things cast a shadow on his mind. One was the still not entirely eradicated fear of the Phantom, and the other was Haslam, standing by his side, his beaming face full of the expectancy of his cut out of the proceeds. Dawlish wondered vaguely why there always had to be something to upset complete equanimity of mind, and the fact that it was all caused by his own ruthlessness in the past never for an instant dawned upon him.

'I think,' Haslam said, as they left the Distribution chief's office, 'that you and I have one or two matters to attend to. The company's on a sound footing now, and likely to remain so.'

'Okay,' Dawlish growled. 'Come along with me to my hotel.'

Once there Dawlish had no alternative but to write a cheque of his own for half the amount he had received. Without a smile he handed it to Haslam.

'Thanks.' Haslam took it and examined it, then put it in his wallet. 'And you have six months in which to repay half the amount it has cost to erect this pipeline.'

'I know,' Dawlish grunted. 'You've put in half of the amount gratis so as to establish yourself as a partner, but the other half has to be repaid. You don't think I'd forget that, do you? It's going to mean I'm working for next to nothing for the next six months, and I'll still have to take care of my overheads or have trouble on my hands.'

'You knew all the conditions of the contract before you signed it, Dawlish. On the whole I think I've been pretty generous.'

'That's a matter of opinion. For a man as wealthy as you you could afford to be less grasping.'

'Business is business whether you've a lot of money or none at all. However, there is always the simple way out of your problem if you wish to take it.'

Dawlish smiled bitterly. 'Sell out my interest to you and let you collect the results of my hard work whilst you've sat on your backside in New Orleans? No, Haslam, I'm not that crazy . . . I realize now that the one mistake I made was in thinking you were my friend.'

'Have it your own way,' Haslam shrugged. 'Nobody's a friend when business has to be transacted. Anyway, think things out. Meantime I'll need a monthly report on how the enterprise is progressing. From the look of this initial start all should be well.'

Upon that Haslam took his departure. Dawlish stood for a long time thinking, his mind endeavouring to recover the earlier nebulous idea he had had concerning an 'accident'. As far as he could see there was now no other way out of the difficulty if he were ever to get himself in the clear. Otherwise Haslam would always be on the doorstep with his hand out.

Gradually, as Dawlish left the hotel and took his final leave of the Distribution chief, the original idea he had had began to reappear in Dawlish's mind. Of course! The Phantom Avenger! He was still a most useful lever and surely there was no reason why he should not strike at Haslam as much as anybody else since he was now connected so closely with Dawlish and the oil enterprise. Clem Dawlish began to feel better. The Phantom Avenger was going to ride again, and to very good purpose.

His plan now fully matured in his mind Dawlish departed from Willard's Acres immediately after lunch, taking care to advertise to everybody that he was going. Then he set off, fully provisioned and supplied, and kept on riding until he was beyond all sight of Willard's Acres. By the time he had accomplished this it was late afternoon. He stopped for a while, watered and rested his horse, and then at length set off again, riding in a wide detour which both took him away from the vicinity of the pipeline and Willard's Acres.

This roundabout procedure meant that in the end he struck the one solitary trail eastwards which Haslam must have taken in order to get back to New Orleans. New Orleans was a long way off and Haslam was not a man who ever hurried anything. Long before he reached his destination Dawlish was quite sure he would catch up with him, despite the time he had been compelled to lose. So he kept on riding relentlessly, only stopping when the absolute exhaustion of his horse made it necessary.

The late afternoon became evening, and the evening night. With the abatement of heat and recovered somewhat after a long rest, Dawlish's horse kept on going, though Dawlish well knew that the animal might easily run itself out before he had overtaken his quarry. It was a risk that had to be taken, and a stern risk it was. The death of a horse in such utterly desolate country could end in tragedy for the rider too.

It was as this disquieting realization took solid form in Dawlish's mind, and he was contemplating a prolonged halt, that he caught a glimpse of something infinitely far ahead of him in the soft darkness of the starry night. It looked like a tiny match flame, but it could just as easily be a fair-sized campfire. It was quite enough for Dawlish. Instead of stopping he urged his stumbling, panting animal to further efforts, and in that he provided the straw which broke the camel's back. Halfway to that solitary point of light the horse stumbled and Dawlish only just succeeded in throwing himself clear in time. He crashed to the sand, struggled up, and then returned to where the animal was now lying full length. In a matter of moments he knew the animal was dead.

'Damn!' Dawlish grunted to himself, and went to work to take his most important belongings from the saddle. It meant he was finally monstrously encumbered, but there was nothing else for it . . . So he presently went on again, stumbling through the sand, cursing his own tiredness, keeping his eye on that dimly flickering light. And suppose it wasn't Haslam at all, at the end of it, but just some trail-hopper passing the night? Well, if so, Dawlish was prepared to fall in with whoever it was and maybe beg a lift. Of one thing he was certain: he would not turn back until he had eliminated Haslam from the scheme of things.

Altogether it was an hour and a half before Dawlish came close enough to the light to study out details. He was satisfied now that it was a campfire, set in a small outcropping of desert scrub so there was plenty of fuel supply. For a while, as he lay in the sand and surveyed Dawlish could not detect anything further — then gradually he descried the outlines of a horse, nodding sleepily, its forelegs hobbled. Nearby, on the opposite side of the fire, a solitary figure lay covered in blankets.

Dawlish grinned to himself. He hadn't come all this way in vain. It was Haslam: the horse itself, a piebald, was identification enough for that. Then the rest was simple.

Carefully Dawlish raised himself on to his knees and drew his right-hand gun, then he crept nearer to his target so there could be no chance of missing. When at last he had manoeuvred into a satisfactory position he took aim.

'Hold it, Dawlish!' a voice said behind him — and instantly he turned his head in shocked amazement. He found himself looking straight into the barrel of a .45. Haslam was standing right behind him, grimly smiling in the campfire light.

'Surprised, eh?' Haslam asked dryly. 'I thought you might be. Leather your gun, Dawlish!'

Dawlish hesitated, which was enough for Haslam. He snatched the gun away and thrust it in his belt. This done he relaxed a little and settled squatting on the sand — but he kept his .45 ready just in case Dawlish might suddenly draw his remaining left-hand gun.

'I'm not a clairvoyant or anything like that,' Haslam explained, 'but I did have a sort of feeling that you might take advantage of a lonely trail to New Orleans to put paid to me. As I worked it, out you'd have every advantage in doing so, though I couldn't quite see who you'd get to take the blame . . . Anyway, that doesn't matter. I'm glad of my hunch. It makes me understand our relationship so much better.'

'Relationship?' Dawlish muttered, wondering why he had not yet got a bullet through him.

'Yeah. You've tried to make yourself out to be so friendly, even though I've had private suspicions of you. I'm glad to know that you're nothing less than a double-crosser anxious to wipe me out. Always as well to know your man.'

'That cuts both ways,' Dawlish growled. 'You'd gain as much advantage by eliminating me, as I would eliminating you. There'd be no more fifty per cent cutting. What the hell are you wasting time talking for when you've got the drop on me?'

'I just don't happen to be a killer, Dawlish: that's the difference between you and me . . . ' Haslam grinned widely in the firelight. 'Nothing like a nice friendly chat under the stars and open sky to clear things up, is there?'

'Oh, shut up!'

'Not just yet. Oh, I put that campfire there as a beacon light in case you did follow me. I was delighted when I saw my guess had been right. The sleeping figure there is a few provision boxes and a water barrel covered by blankets.'

Dawlish said nothing but his left hand began to stray down to his gun.

'I'm glad to know how we stand, Dawlish, because I can be on my guard. I might add that none of it surprises me because I have never trusted you from the first moment I set eyes on you all those years ago — And keep your left hand up! That's better! Now, let's get this straight. We're partners and I intend to stick to my legal side of the contract. And I'm not going to hurt a hair of your pretty head, nor even kill you. I'm not that kind of a man.'

Dawlish breathed a little more freely even though he could not quite grasp Haslam's peculiar magnanimity.

'What I am going to do is try something much more lingering — more painful if you like, especially to a man like you who loves money so much. I'm going to squeeze you, Dawlish, and squeeze again, and again. I'm going to make you run an oil empire that, no matter what you do, never pays you a handsome dividend. I'm going to make financial demands on you that will make you writhe, all of them in a legal framework — demands I am entitled to make since I put up the money for the enterprise. My lawyer knows exactly how far I can go if I choose to be exacting. And exacting I am going to be. If you grow sickened with your financial obligations to me you can always sell out.'

Dawlish got slowly to his feet, reassured by now that no physical attack was contemplated. Haslam rose too and put his gun back in its holster.

'Now we understand each other completely,' he said.

'Completely,' Dawlish assented. 'The

most uneasy partners that ever were. You've said what you're going to do, but since you also know the kind of man I am you don't expect I'll lie down to it do you? I'll pull every trick I know to rid myself of you.'

'I fully expect that, but I don't think you'll catch me napping, Dawlish . . . Now, where's your horse?'

'Dead. I overran it. Why do you think I'm carrying all this stuff with me?'

'All right, we'll stay here for the night. You can sleep if you want to. I shan't, for obvious reasons. Tomorrow we'll carry on to New Orleans, and the first town we come to you'll get yourself a fresh horse and then head homeward. After that, things will go on as before — almost. By the time another dividend from the oil comes round you'll see how much I'm capable of.'

★   ★   ★

It was towards noon next day when the two men, astride the one horse, rode

218

into the little township of Hell's Bend, some twenty miles from where they had held their midnight rendezvous. Here Dawlish was compelled to buy another horse, then he and Haslam parted without a word, partners in name only, sworn enemies at heart.

And, in a black mood, Dawlish rode throughout the day, turning over all kinds of impossible schemes in his mind, until by nightfall he finally arrived back at the Carterville Oil Centre.

The first man to greet him as he wearily wandered into his headquarters office hut was Lincoln. It seemed to make matters even worse to Dawlish to behold the engineer smiling all over his face.

'Glad to see you back, Mr Dawlish. I was wondering where you'd gotten to when you didn't follow me yesterday from Willard's Acres. I'd sorta hoped we'd make the journey together.'

'I had things to do which made it impossible for me to follow on immediately.' With an effort Dawlish dragged himself to awareness. 'Well, how are things going on here? Okay?'

'Everything's just fine and you sure weren't wrong in the way you assessed the oil in this region. It's packed tight and flowing over . . . ' The engineer gave a serious smile. 'We're going to make a fortune, Mr Dawlish — all of us — and there's nobody but you you've got to thank for it. In a few years this area is going to make Carterville one of the wealthiest oil producing organizations in the world.'

'Mmm, I surely hope so,' Dawlish muttered, rubbing his stubbly chin. 'Sorry if I seem a little doped,' he added. 'I've had a hard, long ride.'

'Yes, I can imagine. Anyway, there's a matter I want to ask you about. We're in need of about fifty more men for the labour group on number three derrick. Have I the okay to engage 'em? They're ready and waiting — men from Carterville itself.'

'Go right ahead. Anything else?'

'No — at least, not in connection

with the oil project. There is another matter which isn't strictly in my province. The people in town are saying that it's about time we had a mayor. Mr Dexter was killed by the Phantom before he could take over that office. How about it? Since Carterville has suddenly started putting itself on the map a responsible townsman is a necessity.'

'Yes, sure enough,' Dawlish acknowledged, thinking. 'We've been too busy so far to think about it. Any nominations?'

'Two, as a matter of fact. Some folks have suggested that your partner, Mr Haslam, might — '

'Definitely not!'

'Oh! . . . ' Lincoln looked vaguely surprised at the curt veto. 'One or two people saw him when he inspected this site, and they — '

'I said no, Lincoln, and I meant it. Besides, he has too many ties in New Orleans to be able to come here. Who's the other nominee?'

'Matter of fact it's myself. As chief engineer around here I have a certain position and — '

'Excellent choice,' Dawlish said promptly. 'You go to work on that, Lincoln, and I'll back you to the hilt. We'll see if we can't hold an election tomorrow evening and get the thing settled. As you say, it's time Carterville got its civic affairs in order since it is likely to become famous.'

So after a day spent in checking over the oil field's resources and future possibilities, Dawlish occupied the following evening in 'pushing' Lincoln into the role of Mayor. It suited him to do so. Lincoln was right on his side, and once elected there would be no further talk of dragging in Haslam to fill the office. Haslam perpetually on the doorstep, and in a position of authority, would have been more than Dawlish could have tolerated.

As things worked out he had his way. His popularity was tops at the moment and there wasn't a man or woman present who wished to offend him — so towards eight o'clock that evening the big engineer had been elected and, in this respect, Dawlish felt his task was finished. He could return now to the deep waters of his thoughts and try and think up some way to push Haslam out of the picture. Meanwhile he lounged near the bar of the Journey's End — in which the election had of course been held — and listened detachedly to the banging of the cash-desk drawer. It all meant money coming in — and if Haslam had his way it meant money going out too. Haslam! There had got to be a way of blotting him out.

'Excuse me, Mr Dawlish. You busy at the moment?'

Dawlish looked up quickly. A tall, heavily built man of late middle-age was standing beside him. A heavy greying beard covered most of his face, and what there was of the face was badly scarred and twisted as though at some time he had been in a violent encounter of some kind. Otherwise, from his voice, he seemed a cut above the average cowpoke or cattle trader.

'What's the trouble?' Dawlish asked, shelving his Haslam plans for a moment.

'I'm one of your new number three derrick workers. Mr Lincoln engaged quite a number of us this morning.'

'I know. What about it?'

'Well, this isn't rightly my business but I think you ought to know about it . . . When did you last examine the top of number three derrick?'

Dawlish shrugged. 'I never did. I leave that kind of thing to Lincoln. He's the chief engineer. Why, is there something wrong with number three?'

'In my opinion, everything. The top structure's unsafe. If we get one of these desert storms, as we do some-times, the top might easily come down and kill somebody. I know a thing or two about derricks; I've been on the job all my life. I was up on number three this afternoon — at the very top — and I certainly didn't like what I saw. Besides, it's dangerous for workers to be up there putting the finishing touches.'

'Well, surely you've reported this to Mr Lincoln?'

'I have, yes, and he made an examination himself — but he says I'm imagining things. That there's nothing wrong.'

'Oh?' Dawlish frowned for a moment. If this worker was right and something did come down with a bang, a good deal of the friendly feeling would vanish. Finally Dawlish waited to catch Mayor Lincoln's eye as he stood near the bar, then he motioned him across.

'Yes, Mr Dawlish?'

Dawlish glanced at the bearded worker. 'What's this, Lincoln, about number three derrick being unsafe?'

'Just plain nonsense,' the engineer answered frankly. 'And I don't know why Edwards here should want to waste your time bringing it to your notice. He reported this so-called danger to me and I made an immediate examination. I can only think he must have been seeing things — else maybe he's getting too old for the altitude.'

'I'm not too old, and I tell you it's unsafe,' Edwards said flatly. 'From halfway up that derrick has just been thrown together and anything might happen.'

'I tell you — ' Lincoln began, then Dawlish cut him short.

'Wait a minute, Lincoln. Edwards seems mighty sure of his ground. I'm not casting any reflection on you because you know your job, but the best of us miss something occasionally. I can't afford to take chances so I'll have a look at the derrick myself first thing in the morning.'

'And if it should collapse in the night?' Edwards asked. 'What then?'

'Oh, this is crazy!' Lincoln exclaimed in amazement. 'There isn't one chance in a million of it — '

'I think there is, Mr Lincoln, with all respect.' Edwards was coldly firm about it. 'Don't forget that the men who guard the oil area have their quarters around each derrick. If number three were to come down through vibratory disturbance or other, or even a sudden night gust from the desert wind, there'd be a devil of a lot of trouble. I say examine the thing now and have done with it.'

'It's still mad,' Lincoln snapped.

'All right, I'll see to it,' Dawlish sighed. 'I'll have a look this moment — but if after all this you're wrong, Edwards, look out for plenty of trouble.'

'Want me too?' Lincoln enquired.

'No. You'd better stay behind here and get acquainted with those you need to know in your capacity as mayor.'

Disgruntled — and indeed not a little annoyed — Dawlish led the way out of the Journey's End and then gave Edwards a glance as he came up beside him.

'Better get the safety belts, Edwards. It's a difficult climb in the dark, especially if the top's as rocky as you seem to think. I'll meet you at number three.'

Edwards nodded and went off into the darkness, heading in the direction of the distant lighted area which marked the oil site. Dawlish took the same direction, more slowly, not at all relishing the dizzying task he had set for himself. It occasioned him a passing surprise when, upon reaching derrick three, looming high above him towards the stars, he beheld no sign of any men on guard. From what he could see in the distance there were the usual watchers around the other derricks, but this particular one was deserted. He was debating whether or not to demand an explanation when Edwards came up out of the gloom, carrying two safety belts in his hand.

'I took the liberty of clearing the guards away, Mr Dawlish, just in case of any trouble,' he explained. 'I thought it wisest. While we're around the derrick's guarded anyway.'

'All told, you seem to be taking one hell of a lot of responsibility on your shoulders,' Dawlish growled. 'Still,

maybe you're right in this instance . . .'
He paused, his attention suddenly caught by a faint gleam of light which appeared to be coming from the midst of the mechanisms which controlled the bore-cap.

'What the devil's that?' he demanded, puzzled. 'There ought not to be any naked light near the bore: it's plain asking for trouble.'

'Would be if the cap were moved,' Edwards admitted, also looking. 'As it is there's no danger. That's the dying remains of the fire the men had whilst they had their supper. It looks to be nearly underneath the derrick, but actually it isn't.'

Dawlish said no more. He was anxious to get the derrick climb over and done with. He took the belt Edwards handed him and together they went forward, coming finally directly beneath the derrick. From this vantage point Dawlish could see that the flickering light was actually some distance away — apparently from some embers which had fanned into life again before expiring. Satisfied there was no danger he buckled the belt around him, tested the safety hook, and then began to climb the short ladder which led into the latticed intricacies of the derrick itself. Below him came Edwards, light fanning from the lamp fastened to his belt.

When presently half the ascent had been completed Dawlish paused, gripping the framework tightly. Below he could still see the flickering remains of that campfire and found himself vaguely wondering how much longer it was going to take to go out. Then he transferred his attention to Edwards as he came clambering up beside him.

'You said the trouble was halfway up,' Dawlish reminded. 'We ought to be about it by now.'

'Higher yet,' Edwards answered shortly, so — with a grim glance — Dawlish continued clambering. He ascended perhaps another fifty feet when his attention was caught by an odd sound. After a second or two he had analysed what it was: the machinery for moving aside the cap to the oil bore.

'What's — what's that noise?' he demanded abruptly, even though he knew what it was.

'The cap lever equipment,' Edwards answered calmly. 'As you know it works automatically so as to give the operator a chance to get clear if he wants to. Takes about five minutes before the mechanism works as a rule.'

'What in hell are you talking about?' Dawlish demanded, panting, as Edwards came up beside him.

'You'll find out,' Edwards said coldly, his manner changing. 'Keep on going, Dawlish — to the top!'

Dawlish stared incredulously, then he started at the sight of a gun in Edwards' right hand. The starlight reflected back from the barrel.

'I said, to the top!' Edwards repeated deliberately.

The only conclusion Dawlish could come to was that Edwards was a lunatic

— but that didn't make the position any better. To go down again was impossible with Edwards barring the way with his gun. To jump for it was equally out of the question. So, commencing to sweat with alarm, Dawlish stumbled higher, still listening to the hum of the cap-machinery below and still seeing that irritating solitary flame from the apparently everlasting campfire.

So finally he reached the narrow flat platform at the top of the derrick. Breathing hard he gripped the rail and waited whilst Edwards climbed up beside him. For a man of his age he seemed surprisingly undisturbed after the climb he had made.

'Now, Mr Dawlish,' he said quietly. 'At last I can make sure that you don't slip away.'

'What the devil are you talking about?' Dawlish demanded in fury. 'What about this derrick? When do we examine it? What's the gun for, anyhow?'

'Come to think of it,' Edwards said thoughtfully, 'the gun doesn't really signify anyhow. Not any more.'

He contemplated it for a moment in the starlight — then with an abrupt movement he threw it out into space. The instant that happened Dawlish took the only chance left to him. He dived for the narrow trap which led to the internal ladder, but a savage blow across the face sent him reeling backwards. He caught at the guard rail around the platform and shook his head dazedly.

'In a few minutes,' Edwards said, in the same cold, calm voice, 'I hope to see the consummation of my scheme of reprisal. Maybe even the destruction of your entire oil enterprise . . . '

Something clicked in Dawlish's mind. He turned slowly, wiping a trickle of blood from his nose.

'The — Phantom!' Dawlish whispered. 'You're the Phantom Avenger!'

'Yes. I said I'd catch up with you finally. Now I've done it. I've trailed you endless times, watched you, even had my gun drawn on you, but somehow you've always got out of reach. So I chose this way. As a worker I saw my chance, and I've taken it ... There's nothing wrong with this derrick. At least not at the moment. Very soon it ought to become your funeral pyre — and mine. Only it doesn't matter about me. With my job done I'm quite prepared to die, rather than be arrested for murder and sabotage.'

'But — '

'You don't know me, do you?' Edwards asked softly. 'Who I really am?'

'No — no, I've never seen you before ... '

'Yes, that's probably true. I don't suppose you had the nerve to ride with the men who destroyed the ranches and killed the owners ... Nobody else has recognized me, either. The beard disguises a lot — and the fire did the rest.'

Dawlish waited, having a clear insight as to how a mouse must feel when a cat stands looking at it.

'My name,' Edwards said, 'is Pedder. That mean anything to you?'

'Pedder — ? The — the Double-Noose Ranch — '

'Exactly — the Double-Noose. The first ranch your blasted hoodlums burned down! My wife and daughter died in the flames, but I managed to get clear. My face suffered the most, as you may have noticed, enough for it to be changed considerably. I escaped up-country and stayed with my brother until I'd recovered. Then I made up my mind to hunt you down and destroy everything you stand for, including the men beside you. I became a Phantom too, this time working against you.'

'You're lying!' Dawlish shouted hysterically. 'You must be! The sheriff found the bones in the ashes of your ranch — They were buried.'

'Did he count them one by one?' Pedder asked venomously. 'Did he build them up rib by rib and account for three bodies? Of course he didn't! He couldn't! He found bones, a few personal possessions, and assumed all three of us had died. But it was only my wife and daughter . . . ' Pedder's tone changed. 'You've never tasted fire, have you, Dawlish? Never felt its awful sting? It's stifling touch — '

'For God's sake take your revenge and get it over with!' Dawlish screamed. 'Don't stand there talking!'

'You've escaped me so long, Dawlish, I must enjoy the sweet pleasure of seeing you writhe — as my wife and daughter writhed in flames they couldn't escape . . . Some would call me mad,' Pedder continued, half to himself. 'Mad from grief and near-death in the fire. But the mad have an evil cunning, and I'm grateful that I'm no exception.'

Dawlish groaned to himself; then suddenly he found his neck and head seized in a steel grip. He was powerless to help himself as Pedder compelled him to look below on the winking spot of that still flickering campfire.

'Naturally you can see that,' Pedder said. 'Let me explain. It isn't a camp-fire. It's a large sized lump of tallow with a wick through it. By now it will have burned down to the limit. When that final point is reached it will ignite a trail of gunpowder which leads to the oil bore of this particular derrick. There wasn't much trouble in arranging it. I cleared the men away first, supposedly at your orders, so I had the field to myself. They won't investigate until it's too late.'

'You've planned to set the well on fire!' Dawlish shouted, tearing free. 'That's what you mean, isn't it?'

'Of course!' Pedder's voice was so bland he sounded surprised that there could be any doubt as to his intentions. 'I knew you would send me for the safety belts, so that was the opportunity I chose. I set the automatic cap mechanism in action. You heard it start up when we were halfway up this derrick. If you listen carefully you'll still hear it. At any moment now the mechanism will swing the cap aside and the oil will gush upwards. Only a few seconds after that — according to the timing I've worked out in these last few weeks — the powder trail will ignite and then — '

'Well . . . ' Pedder's voice changed again. 'You too will feel the sting of flames, Dawlish. So will I, but that doesn't matter any more. Possibly this whole oil region will catch fire and wipe out everything you've fought for. The — '

Dawlish could stand no more. He slammed out his right fist, aiming straight for Pedder's jaw. Pedder staggered a little but quickly recovered himself. He dived for the frantically struggling figure of Dawlish as he tried to get down to the ladder . . . For the second time he failed. He was seized, hauled up by a madman's strength, and then slammed backwards by blow after blow until he collapsed on his knees.

Then, suddenly, the mechanism below

operated. There was a noise like steam escaping a jet, followed in a matter of seconds by an upwardly climbing deluge of oil. Pedder laughed out loud as the flood enveloped him. Dawlish tried to get up and slithered down again, plastered in oil from head to foot, hardly able to see, the stuff running into his mouth and blinding his eyes.

'Oil!' Pedder screamed. 'The filthy stuff you killed and maimed to get, Dawlish! How d'you like it — but the best has yet to come!'

What happened then the hapless Dawlish did not know — but to the startled men at the neighbouring derricks some distance away there was no doubt about it. The roar of the oil gusher was the first thing that attracted them and for a second or two they stood in amazement watching that dark, curving pillar against the stars — then came something else. There was a flash of flame and a mighty outwardly bursting bubble of ignited oil. In split seconds the entire jetting column was on fire, igniting the derrick, and discharging densely thick rollers of smoke to the sky. Pedder's wick and tallow had been nicely timed.

Fire!

Instantly the men began moving, entirely unaware that at the top of the derrick Dawlish and Pedder were at that very moment perishing in the holocaust of flame which enveloped them ... The news of the fire hardly needed sending to Carterville: there were plenty in the main street who saw it begin and in seconds the news had reached the Journey's End. Instantly there was hurried movement, with engineer Lincoln at the head of it. He went through the batwings at top speed and, followed by the men who had been in the saloon, headed for the oil area. As he ran he appraised the situation. Number three derrick was plainly a dead loss. It was nothing more now than a blazing skeleton with the fiery column shooting up its centre. Long before Lincoln had reached the site the whole tower crumbled and tottered in a fantastic mass of sparks and torches ... And the main ignited oil fountain remained.

On the site itself Lincoln found the men swinging the fire-fighting equipment into action. Immediately he raced across to them.

'Never mind that!' he directed. 'The other derricks are not to windward of the sparks and the caps are closed. We've got to get the cap back on that damned thing — Come on!'

Immediately the men obeyed his orders, approaching with a slowing tread as they began to feel the terrific heat from the blazing oil. When they had reached the limit of advancement Lincoln stopped and glanced around him.

'Fire suit — quick!' he ordered, and within seconds the clumsy asbestos outfit with its helmet was brought forward. He struggled into it, waited impatiently whilst the helmet was put in position, and then began to advance again.

Knee-deep in embers he kept on going until he had reached the mechanism which operated the cap lever. It was out of action since once it had swung the cap aside it had automatically cut out — nor, despite all Lincoln's efforts, would it start up again. The heat had evidently thrown the works out of action.

Lincoln looked about him warily. There was still part of the burning derrick poised dangerously above him. It might last a long time; it might come down any moment. He had to take that chance. Making up his mind he grabbed the long lever of the cap, detached the bar which linked it to the mechanism, and then began to swing the lever inwards, directing the cap nearer and nearer to that bright flaming point above the bore where the gushing oil had ignited. Twice he manoeuvred, and missed. Then the third time he plunged the cap squarely home. Instantly the fire died, snuffed out from lack of air.

Breathing hard, Lincoln came stumbling

back to where the men were standing in the starlight. Some of them were cheering his lone-hand effort; others were dragging the stuffy helmet and suit away from him. At last he was free and, mopping his face, he glanced around him.

'What happened to Mr Dawlish and Edwards?' he asked.

The men looked at each other, puzzled.

'Mr Dawlish? Why, was he supposed to be here?'

'Of course he was!' Lincoln looked amazed. 'He came with Edwards to examine number three derrick. You remember the fuss Edwards kicked up this morning because he thought that derrick was unsafe — ?'

'Wait a minute!' Another man came forward. 'Edwards was here because I was with a few boys around derrick three. Edwards told us Dawlish had given orders that we were to keep away from the derrick. So naturally we moved on. The next thing we knew the oil had started gushing. Then came the fire.'

Lincoln was silent for a long moment; then he sighed.

'I don't think you need say anything more. What we've been witnessing boys is, I think, the last act of the Phantom Avenger. Remember, he said he would get Dawlish finally, and we can be pretty sure that he succeeded and killed himself in the doing. The whole thing was obviously planned, and it was so devised that sabotage came into it as well.'

'Yeah,' one of the men muttered. 'It could have been the Avenger at that.'

'I'm convinced of it.' Lincoln looked back towards the debris. 'Who he was I guess we shan't ever know . . . Well, we still have the oil yield and I'm still chief engineer. All I can do is report to Mr Haslam what has happened. He's the remaining partner, so it's up to him now. In my other capacity as mayor I'll report this whole business to the nearest authorities and tell them it is my belief that the Avenger is dead.'

And Lincoln, next day, did exactly

that. When Haslam eventually got the news, just as he was upon the point of closing his office, he listened in silence to all Lincoln had to say. Not by the merest trace of expression did he betray his feelings at hearing of the death of his partner.

'So I guess the responsibility for the enterprise is yours, from here on, sir,' Lincoln said, shrugging. 'I assume all orders will henceforth come from you.'

'Correct,' Haslam agreed. 'I'll make arrangements to be in Carterville very shortly — Oh, I assume there will be some kind of token funeral for Mr Dawlish?'

'There will be, yes — as a matter of respect even though there are no remains to be found.'

'I see. Make arrangements for a large wreath to be bought and upon it have a card saying 'Gone, but not Forgotten' will you? Add my name. You have my sanction.'

'Yes, sir. I'll do that. I'll be in Carterville when you need me.'

On that Lincoln departed. Haslam sat thinking for a moment, then he snipped the end from a cigar and grinned widely to himself.

THE END

We do hope that you have enjoyed reading this large print book.

Did you know that all of our titles are available for purchase?

We publish a wide range of high quality large print books including:
Romances, Mysteries, Classics
General Fiction
Non Fiction and Westerns

Special interest titles available in large print are:
The Little Oxford Dictionary
Music Book, Song Book
Hymn Book, Service Book

Also available from us courtesy of Oxford University Press:
Young Readers' Dictionary
(large print edition)
Young Readers' Thesaurus
(large print edition)

For further information or a free brochure, please contact us at:
Ulverscroft Large Print Books Ltd.,
The Green, Bradgate Road, Anstey,
Leicester, LE7 7FU, England.
Tel: (00 44) **0116 236 4325**
Fax: (00 44) **0116 234 0205**

When Jake Probyn hauls up outside the Circle F ranch, he's looking for work, not trouble. But he finds trouble in the shape of the boss's daughters and the foreman, Ransome. Things get worse when the old man dies leaving the ranch to his daughters. Then there are back shootings, range fires and one daughter goes missing . . . and while the Drowned Valley on Circle F land has its own eerie story to tell, there's trouble galore waiting for Jake . . .